Steve Monosson

THE
BALLAD
OF
PIE
CHART
JOHN

PART ONE:
CHARTING THE COURSE

◐ ◐ ◑

☾ CALISTO EDITIONS • NEW YORK ☽

The Ballad of Pie Chart John • Part One: Charting The Course.

©Steve Monosson 2014. All rights reserved.

Edited by Todd Johnson

This book is set in Adobe Garamond Pro.
Titles set in Neutra Text and Display.

Special Limited Edition printed for
Stagecoach Run Arts Festival, Treadwell, NY, June 2014.

This book is dedicated
to all those who have
enjoyed and supported
my work over the years.

◐ ◑ ◒

When I look at a pie chart, I just go numb.

Aaron Koblin
Multimedia Artist

I

HEAD
TO TOE

◗

I N THE BEGINNING, THROUGH the dawn of man and beyond, things
went largely as documented by those who took interest in such
things, as begun in the Age of Reason and continued in successive
eras. Of course there was a good amount of misreading of the historical
record, and not a few outlandish hypotheses managed to gain general
acceptance. Furthermore, there were many well-intentioned plans
spawned in an effort to unite humanity in a common good, schemes
which only served to divide it further.

But we're getting ahead of ourselves here; more on the big picture
stuff later.

For now, let us concern ourselves with a skinny, tenuously adjusted
ten-year-old boy in the suburbs of Cleveland, Ohio, circa 1972. 1972 came
long after the beginning, whether one defines the starting line from the
scientific point of view or from the more traditional, faith-based one.
Regardless of which school of thought one attends, it is inarguable that
in the year in question a ten-year-old boy could find himself occupied
with a tanned pigskin stitched with such ingenuity and precision that it
could be inflated, and this object would be called a football. And this is
where our story begins.

John Keller was such a boy, easily lost to everything around him to the
inexhaustible turnings of his inner thought processes. He might wander
off in his head for minutes on end and miss the bus to school while
examining a flyer for a garage sale tacked to a telephone pole, trying to
gauge from the composition and general tone of the flyer what were his
chances of finding therein an undiscovered copy of the Declaration of
Independence.

In the middle of putting on his shoes he might find himself so absorbed with mentally alphabetizing all rock bands known to him whose name began with the letter "S" that he would often fail to properly outfit his feet, donning the second shoe from a different, unmatched pair. But most of all, John lost track of the world with his head ensconced in a selection of randomly gathered books. A reading of *Robinson Crusoe* might be followed by one on the history of fertilizer.

"What the hell do you want to know about fertilizer?" his father would ask. "Are you starting a cornfield somewhere?"

"I don't know," was John's typical and genuine response, shrugging his shoulders and wandering off.

After one such exchange, John's father, Marvin Keller, a man in his mid-forties with a penchant for having several unfinished household projects going at once, turned to his wife in frustration.

"June, I want him to do something physical. If that kid's head was a TV, it would always be stuck on some foreign channel with lousy reception."

"What do you suggest, Marv?"

"Hell, I always loved football. That's got to be in him somewhere. I'm gonna dig out that football from the pile in the garage and see what happens."

"What—do you expect him to sprout shoulder pads?"

Marvin Keller didn't answer his wife but instead headed for the garage to dig in the corner through a jungle of old golf clubs, garden hoses to be repaired, broken Christmas tree lights which were always on the list to be fixed but had been out of service for several Christmases running, and similar refuse which had yet to be formally declared as such and taken to the dump. At last, underneath the rolled up and irreparably torn lawn water slide, Marvin found the only viable item in the pile and what he was looking for: a brown leather football. The football had been a gift for John at his birth, and was relegated to the should-be-junk pile as there was no card indicating who had presented the gift. It was assumed that the card had been lost, and the Kellers were too embarrassed to inquire of friends and family as to who was the donor.

Marvin Keller dusted off the football and headed out of the garage. He found John on the back porch reading an old Zane Grey western. Marvin spun the football around in his hands.

"Hey son."

"Hey pop."

"How about you and me havin' a catch?"

"A catch? With that?" Just the sight of his father passing the ball back and forth between his hands made John uneasy.

"No—with a rock. C'mon, we'll have fun."

"Fun? I don't know—"

"Oh come on," said Marvin Keller, "go out for a pass!"

"What do you mean?" said John.

"What do you mean 'what do you mean?' Sometimes you act like you're from Mars. Start running and I'll hit you with a pass."

"Okay." So John put down his book and started running toward the rear of the backyard. His father tossed a perfectly timed spiral that John reeled in with outstretched arms, doing so with fair athletic grace.

"Whoa—lookin' good, son. Now toss it back."

"What?"

"Throw me back the ball."

"Why?"

"That's how a catch works."

"But I caught it already."

It was at times like this that Marvin Keller had trouble believing that this was his flesh and blood offspring. "Let's get a rhythm going, son. Let's see how good you are."

"How many times do I have to catch the ball?"

"'Have to?' This is fun, kiddo."

"Oh, I see. Well, I guess I'm having fun," said John honestly, "but do you think we can stop after I make ten catches?"

Pausing to toss the ball back and forth again between his hands, Marvin Keller felt frustration mixed with the satisfaction of seeing his son do something athletic. He measured his words before speaking. "Just ten catches, huh? Well, I guess it's a start. Maybe we'll do fifteen next time, what do you say?"

"Maybe, pop. I'll think about it." John smiled, and his father smiled in return.

At the completion of the session, Marvin hailed John from across the yard. "I'll see you later, son. Got some work around the house to catch up on. You hold on to that ball, get a good feel for it."

So Marvin Keller disappeared into the house through the back door, leaving John to release the football and let it drop to the ground in front of him.

John felt a momentary impulse to return to his Zane Grey western, but before he could do so, he did something unexpected, something spontaneous. He picked the ball back up and soon found himself tossing it between his hands with some enthusiasm, much like his father. He then carefully took his foot to the ball and punted it straight up, watching it rise some fifteen feet in the air. When it landed near the trashcans by the back door, he ran with what might be interpreted as enthusiasm to retrieve it. He then repeated this for the rest of the afternoon. June Keller took notice of John's new activity, looking out from the kitchen window.

"Marv, come here. You're not going to believe this," she said.

"What?" Marvin Keller was finally fixing the two kitchen drawers that didn't close without considerable effort.

"Come see what your son is doing."

Marvin Keller got off of his knees and out from under the drawer to join his wife at the window.

"Would you look at that," he said.

The couple silently watched their son punt the ball to himself back and forth across the yard for another ten minutes, which is when John quit and returned to his book. The Kellers stood where they were for another few moments.

"Do you think I should say something to him?" asked Marvin Keller.

"No, just let him be. Let's see where this goes."

Where it would go was somewhere neither Keller could have ever imagined.

Each day when he returned from school, John would punt the ball around the yard for a half hour or more. He had no real concept as to how his actions fit into the actual game, nor did he care. He just liked the activity. Eventually, he got so adept at what he was doing that he began to kick the ball far over the fence with regularity. The back of the house was no longer room enough for his kicks. When he shattered the neighbor's window across the street, giving their lhasa apso what would turn out to be a permanent nervous condition as it had been sleeping directly beneath the glass, he was asked to take his game down to the park.

At the park Ted Gelosi, the high school gym coach, got a look at John's punting skills. Gelosi was a heavyset man who was rarely if ever seen out of his worn brown sweat suit. Upon seeing John kick, Gelosi immediately sought to enroll John in the local Punt, Pass, & Kick competition. Coach Gelosi sought to impress John by informing him that none other than Legs Lahoolie, the punter for the Browns, would be judging the contest.

"Legs Lahoolie is the best punter the Browns have had since I was a kid and Mo Freiberg was kicking for them," said the coach.

"But who are the Browns?" John asked.

"Why, they're your hometown team, my boy! I mean, can't you see my shirt?"

"Your shirt says 'Property of The Cleveland *Brows*.'"

It was true. Along with the lettering made hardly legible from a thousand washings, Gelosi had physically worn away the "N" in "BROWNS" through a nervous habit he had of rubbing that spot on his chest with the palm of his hand. Gelosi pulled his shirt down and out from his body to get a good look at the lettering.

"Well would you look at that? It sure does look like the Cleveland 'Brows', now don't it? Maybe it's time for a new sweatshirt, don't you think Johnny?"

"May-bee." John smiled.

The coach slapped John on the shoulder. "*May-bee* is right! And you're gonna win that contest next Saturday and we're all gonna get new shirts—signed by Legs Lahoolie, no less!"

"That'd be cool, coach."

"All right. Tell your folks to have you down at the school at 8am."

John probably would have won the competition if he ever got the chance to kick. During the warm-up John's competitors were mostly engaged in watching Legs Lahoolie punting the ball over half the length of the field. Lahoolie was having the children fetch his punts, which he would re-launch each time saying "Now get a load of this one, half-pints!" This was followed by "oohs" and "ahhs" of those children not already downfield retrieving his previous kicks.

John, meanwhile, was practicing on his own, some twenty yards away. He launched his own bomb of a kick, except he made contact with the ball far too late, which sent the ball sailing high up and back over his head and behind him. Never taking his eye off the ball, John zigzagged under the falling pigskin, hoping to catch it, making a diving catch if necessary. But his failure to concern himself with his immediate surroundings would be his undoing, as he was so focused on his task that he neglected to spy Lahoolie directly in his path. And so "Now get a load of this one, half-pints!" would be the last thing John would hear for some time, as Lahoolie drove his foot straight into John's lunging head.

At the hospital, his parents prayed and sweated the hours as John lay unconscious and clinging to life, comforted little by visits from John's doctors.

"And if he lives, doctor, will he be all right?"

"There's no real way of telling, Mrs. Keller. The left side of his cerebral cortex took an extremely bad hit. The cerebral cortex is critical when it comes to things like memory, attention, perceptual awareness and language. So John's brain could be impacted in a thousand different ways."

June Keller stood up. An otherwise unemotional woman in her forties with a long lean face and frame, she was now venting a lifetime of worry in regard to her son's fate. She played out in her mind the chain of events leading up to the current crisis.

"Why'd you ever have to show him that football? I knew it was a bad idea—I knew it!"

"What are you talking about?" answered Marvin Keller. "The kid loved to kick. Who'd have ever imagined—"

"Don't say 'loved' like he's already gone!"

"Okay, okay. He loves it," said Marvin Keller. "He *loves* it."

But that wasn't actually true anymore. Even in his comatose state, John had lost his affection for punting a football. In the inner recesses of his mind he wondered what activity did hold his interest now, but he couldn't think of a thing. He was intrigued by his state of unconsciousness, though. It was more fascinating than anything else he had experienced in his ten plus years, even that trip to Bermuda three years ago when he narrowly escaped getting bitten by a shark. But he also recognized that it worried his parents to remain comatose, and consequently directed his thoughts to returning to a waking state. But as hard as he tried—and he gave it considerable effort—he could not rouse himself. A combination of physical injury and an irresistible urge to stay where he was kept him unconscious. So he lay down on the floor of his mind to think long and not very hard about nothing in particular. His only thought was that he might enjoy a book right now, though he wasn't sure. Reading might be a challenge in the murky recesses of the deepest part of his mind.

As he lay there experiencing an odd and lazy sensation of comfort, he noticed a twinkling light at the periphery of his vision, exponentially getting brighter and larger with each passing minute. As it neared, the light assumed the shape of a fireball heading straight for him, and John could only lift himself from the floor of his mind to get a better look before the flaming sphere landed without violence, suffusing into John's head in a volcanic and silent burst. The interaction between the orb and John's head sent him into a staggering delirium, which kept him from all but missing the following exchange.

"It's done," said one disembodied male voice.

"Yah. Zat's good!" said another voice, this one with a heavy German accent. "Zo, ven do you zink he vill be ready to do ziss verk for us? Tomorrow? Next veek?"

"Try not to be a moron. It's going to take years."

"Years? Zat's crazy! Vee need him right now!"

"Shut up. Don't make me slap you again. Things need time to develop. I've waited countless millennia. A few more years won't matter."

"Vell, okay. Ziss is your show."

With that, John felt a sudden updraft, and then his mind went calm. Recalling the unclear voices while experiencing that inner turbulence, he listened intently for any further conversation. Hearing nothing further, he felt a new urgency to return to the conscious world. Now when he sat up, he witnessed his environment change around him from within to without, an inner, dark world passing away and his hospital room coming into focus. Recognition of his parents seated to the left of him came next, and then feeling his mother tightly holding onto his hand.

John then opened his eyes wide, turned his htead, and smiled at his mother.

"Oh my god, it's a miracle!" cried June Keller. "Are you okay, my beautiful boy?! I'm so happy, Johnny, say something to me, son. Say something!"

A moment passed before John could think of an appropriate response.

"Hi Mom," he said.

2

FISH
STORY

◑

ALTHOUGH JOHN MADE A remarkable and quick recovery from
his run-in with the foot of Legs Lahoolie, he was not one
hundred percent the same boy he was before the accident.
For one, he exhibited an even greater propensity to catalogue everything
he saw. Being that John's injury was so serious—no matter what the
outcome—that it was recommended he attend a camp for adolescents
who had experienced severe brain trauma. And so in the summer of 1973,
the boy found himself at Camp WeeKoHonus, where it was hoped he
might lose some of his idiosyncratic behavior through association with
other youths who had suffered a similar setback.

"Maybe if people didn't treat the kid like he was from Mars then
maybe he'll come out of his shell some," said Marvin Keller the night
before John was to leave for camp.

"Like you're one to talk," said June Keller. "You're the one who said
his head was like a broken TV set."

"I never said that."

"We were sitting right here and you said that only a month or so
before the accident."

Marvin Keller tapped his fingers on the table, looked down at the
kitchen floor and then back up at his wife seated across the table.

"Okay—I said it. You got me. But I said it with affection."

"Some affection." The accident and subsequent rehab of their son had
put an undeniable strain on the Kellers' marriage.

John went off to the camp the next day, and to some extent the
family got what they were hoping for in WeeKoHonus. Nobody saw
John as special there. In fact, he all but faded into the background of
daily life on the camp within days of his arrival. Many of the campers
required special attention just to get from place to place, their worlds

too private and shaken even for someone like John to relate to. So, not needing dedicated assistance, he was given an informal license to do what he pleased.

John came to relish the time he was allotted each day to go freely about his business—"Hobby Time," as it was called. During this period, campers signed up for their favorite activity, choosing something from the general roster of pastimes. Only during the initial Hobby Time period was John assigned an activity—tennis. The tennis instructor was Arthur Menendez, a man who had competed in the US Open some thirty years ago and had since never stopped talking about his one appearance. Unfailingly, Menendez would embellish his recollection of his only match and quick defeat in the opening round. In his telling, he fought his way to the final match, only to ultimately lose to champion Bobby Riggs in five grueling sets. Sometimes he would go so far as to say that the match was decided on a disputed call, challenging campers "to go look it up," knowing full well that there was no such record available at WeeKoHonus.

Menendez singled John out for his ability to consistently hit the ball over the net. This had the dual effect of drawing to John unwanted attention and alienating his less successful co-campers.

"You suck, suckface." Jimmy Leonard, one of John's bunkmates who was dealing with the aftermath of a serious car accident, and who had not been able to get the ball over the net all afternoon, spit his words at John. The boy then tossed his tennis racquet in frustration at the perimeter fence. John watched the racquet hit high up on the fence, almost scaling it entirely. Seeing this, John wondered why Jimmy had such difficulty negotiating the net if he could achieve such altitude with the racquet. But this meditation was cut short as John felt Jimmy's ire, and he didn't like it in the least. Communication was a chore enough; outright derision he had no stomach for whatsoever.

Unsurprisingly, John declined to use his Hobby Time allotment to engage in any official camp diversion. What John did during Hobby Time was sparked by what he saw during a swimming session at the lake on the second day of camp. There, John had caught a caught a glimpse of three foot-and-a-half long brown fish with darker brown vertical stripes feeding in the shallows. He would learn from a fishing handbook he borrowed from the camp library that these were smallmouth bass. Reading about these bass by flashlight at night, he found it hard to sleep wondering how often the bass returned to the shallows, and if he might see them again the next day.

So when it came time at the breakfast table to choose which activity he would engage in during Hobby Time later that afternoon, John eagerly marked the box at the bottom of the list that read "OTHER," and handed it back to his counselor, Frank. Frank Greenberg was an affable enough young man of nineteen, a head trauma survivor himself, former camper, and psychology student at Ohio State. John's remoteness had not escaped him, and he took this opportunity to get to know his charge a little better.

"John, can you come up here for a minute?" Frank called to John.

"Sure." John shrugged his shoulders, stood up from his seat, and walked around the table to where Frank was seated. His fellow campers hardly heeded his presence; for them he had already faded into the woodwork of their bunk, garnering little more attention than the hooks beneath their cubbies where they hung their jackets.

Frank put his hand on John's shoulder, turning his chair to the side to have a semi-private discussion.

"How are you doing this morning, John?"

"I'm okay."

"Do you like it here at WeeKoHonus?"

"I guess."

"I haven't been able to spend as much time with you as I would like. Your bunkmates have taken up most of my time."

"That's okay. I'm fine by myself."

"I know. But I would like you to work on your social skills."

"That's what my dad always says." There was a pause as John turned his gaze downward at his now slowly shuffling feet.

Greenberg plowed ahead, aiming to draw John back into the conversation. "What things do you like to do?"

Frank's interest was genuine. John sensed that and made an effort to give as honest an answer as he could.

"Umm… the lake. I'd like to go to the lake."

"Do you like to swim?"

"Not really."

"Boating, then?"

"I don't think so. Though I did read a book on the history of shipbuilding."

"I see. So then what are you planning to do at Hobby Time? I see on the form here that you've checked 'OTHER,' but you didn't fill in the blank next to it specifying what you were going to do." Frank showed the paper to John, who took it from Frank's hands.

John put the paper on the table, took the pen which was next to the stack of completed forms, wrote "Lake" on the line next to "OTHER," and gave the form back to his counselor.

"Are you making fun of me, John?"

"No. I'm just going down to the lake. I like being there."

Frank didn't know exactly what to make of John, but then few people did. "Well, I guess that's all right. Just promise me you'll stay within the supervised area."

"Sure. I'll be right next to the dock."

John went to the lake that afternoon, where he took up an instant vigil at the spot where he had seen the three smallmouth bass the previous day. Once he had seen the fish come and go twice over a fifteen-minute period, he took to calculating how many bass he would see if he stood there for a year. He began to factor in darkness, swimmers scaring away the fish, the lake freezing over, trips to the nearest outhouse, his need for sleep, his need to eat, his inability to remain standing where he was due to lightning storms and sub-zero temperatures, conversations with persons inquiring as to why he was standing in the same spot for so long a period of time, etc. As it so happened, one such conversation occurred before he could stand even one hour figuring his fish statistics.

Gretchen Sweeney, a skinny, freckled, red-headed girl John's age, walked up to the boy by the side of the lake and stood beside him for several minutes before he took notice of her. Her parents, professional worriers both, had sent her to the camp as a precautionary measure. That spring she had fallen off her bicycle while not wearing a helmet. The damage was minimal to undetectable as diagnosed by three different doctors, but her parents could not bypass such a golden opportunity to make themselves miserable. They would have preferred she stay home that summer so they could personally monitor her activity. But after hearing about the camp from one of her doctors, she pressed her parents to go there so as to escape their interminable queries as to how she was feeling. Her parents agreed, apprehensive but confident that the camp would report even the slightest sign of dysfunction.

And so at the camp it was determined in short order by the medical staff that there was no real damage to Gretchen's brain. Thus she, like John, had no use for the special attention needed by those less fortunate. Unlike John, Gretchen quickly assumed the role of junior assistant counselor. She sought to be of aid and lent a much needed hand in the comings and goings of her bunkmates. She was more than happy to do what she could to help—it was like playing house and she got to be the mom. But this relationship also left her feeling isolated and somewhat empty, as well. She often just wanted to be an eleven-year-old kid. Her counselors recognized this, and she was given ample free time to roam about and do whatever struck her fancy. Because of this she was free to wander down to the waterfront one afternoon, where she discovered a boy approximately her age so absorbed in some inscrutable lakeside ceremony that a verbal cue was needed to break his concentration. Not even the sounds of her loudly sucking on a bright green lollipop were enough to get the boy's attention.

"Whatcha doin'?" she asked, puzzled, twirling the lolly pop in her right hand.

Ripped from his reverie, John flinched, visibly unsettled for a moment. "What? Oh, hi. Yes, it *is* a very nice lake."

"I didn't ask you what kinda lake it was."

"No?"

"Nope."

John nervously tapped the side of his cheek. "But you asked me something, right?"

"I sure did. I asked you what you were doin'. I been here for like five minutes watchin' you lookin' at the lake and countin' out things on your fingers. I tried to figger it out myself, but you got me stumped." There was nothing but curiosity in her tone.

"Really?" People rarely asked John what he was doing. Most often people would ask him to quit his activity and join the conversation at hand. He thought for a moment as to how to best summarize his lakeside tabulations. He attached great importance to his response as he felt himself suddenly smitten with the ingenuousness of this bony red-headed girl. Her galaxy of freckles, khaki shorts, dirty blue flip flops and inquisitive manner all combined to register deep in John's core to create a favorable impression no other human ever had. It was like she was the answer to some equation John hadn't realized he was desperately trying to figure out.

"I was looking at the fish," he said, finally.

"What fish?" John looked out at the shallows and saw there was indeed nothing but aquatic flora currently visible. "Well, they're not here right now, but smallmouth bass appear pretty often. I'm trying to figure out exactly how often they show up."

"Why would anybody wanna do that?" Gretchen's question was an innocent one. John's instant appreciation of her sincerity left him bordering on speechless.

"Well, well, why not?" John said, shrugging his shoulders and trying not to sound defensive. There was a moment of silence before Gretchen responded.

"Yeah all right. Why not why not?" Gretchen giggled, which loosened John up so that he began to chuckle as well. Gretchen then stuck up her right hand to wave a quick goodbye. "Okay. See ya." She put the lollipop back in her mouth.

"But where are you going?" John surprised himself with how much he was disappointed with the girl's sudden departure.

"Oh, I'm just checkin' out different stuff around this place," she said around the sucker. "You and your fish are tops so far. Are you here all the time?"

"Well, most days at Hobby Time."

"Cool. It's kinda nutty what you're doin'. But everything's kinda nutty around here, don't cha think?"

"Um, I guess so."

"I guess so is right. Then I'll see you tomorrow maybe." Gretchen skipped off, taking out the green lolly and twirling it in her left hand, innocently singing "Jeremiah was a bullfrog…," the opening line from "Joy To The World," the Three Dog Night hit of a couple of summers back. John's attention lingered as he followed Gretchen heading up the hill back to the main camp. He did not return to his study until the girl was well out of sight. Even then he found it hard to concentrate, suddenly finding the green frogs floating amidst the algae of heightened interest.

John returned to the lake the next day at Hobby Time. As much as he tried to focus on his fish, he could not help but wonder if the red-headed girl would return. The on-schedule appearance of the bass trio did little to lift his feelings. After the familiar group had departed, a new fish appeared in the shallows, a smallmouth with odd, bright yellow stripes. Before John could conjecture as to whether or not that this was a mutant strain of smallmouth or a new, hitherto unobserved species, he found himself caught up in a sort of daydream; one involving this fish. The fish appeared to John as if it was hovering in one spot, and was now staring him straight in the eye.

"So vhat are you go-ink to do if she doesn't come back?" John imagined the fish questioning him with a cold impartiality.

"I don't know. I guess I'll be okay," he stared back in response.

"But you like her."

"I guess."

"Don't guess. It is not zeh province of science."

"What does that mean?" The fish's last statement not only confused John, but it also sounded as if he had actually heard it out loud.

"It means zat you better stop vurrying about silly girls and verk on shaping up your brain!"

That statement was not only unmistakably audible, but was scolding and spoken in a thick German accent. John fled the waterside, and would only calm down an hour later, doing all he could to attribute the experience to his injury and his dalliance with daydreaming.

As John was back at the bunk trying to figure out what had just happened, the fish which had spoken to John lingered in the shallows with its eyes rolling nervously. It was soon joined by a largemouth bass almost twice its size. The largemouth addressed the fish who had spoken to John.

"If you ever pull a stunt like that again, I am going to rip your face off, put it back on, and rip it off again."

"Please don't. It hurtz ven you do zat. Acch, does it hurt."

"I know. And to top it off, I will do it slowly. Very, very slowly."

"I understand. I get impatient, zat's all. I vould sink you'd understand zat."

The largemouth bass dipped his head to the bed of the lake and scooped up a mouthful of mud, sand, and pebbles. He swum around to position himself head-to-head with the smallmouth, who was now wildly oscillating his fins and rolling his eyes, holding his position in the water. The larger fish then fired his mouth's contents at the other's face, scraping the smaller fish's eyes and temporarily clogging his gills. The smaller did his all not to show his duress, remaining in his spot.

"That's just a small taste of my displeasure," said the largemouth, "and you can knock off the facing-the-pain-bravely routine. Let's go."

A cloud of smoke materialized beneath the water, accompanied by a faint acrid odor on the surface. When the lake was clear again, the two fish had vanished completely.

3
THE NAME GAME

◐

THE NEXT DAY, JOHN was back by the lake at Hobby Time. He had resolved not to let the prior day's incident interfere with his schedule. He couldn't see explaining to the red-headed girl that the reason he wasn't at the lake to meet her was that he was freaked out that a fish had scolded him and told him to get his brain in shape. No, he wasn't going to dwell on whatever it was that happened the day before.

"Howdy. How's fish food city goin' today?"

Gretchen's question startled John, who was ten minutes into recording data. Nearly dropping his pad, John looked up and smiled.

"Hi. Good to see you—I mean, things are good. Really good."

"Gee, I guess things are good," said Gretchen, winking at John and then peering into the water, her hands clasped behind her back. "But what I don't see, and what I haven't seen yet, are these fish of yours."

"No?" John's heart sank with the possibility that the bass were done with visiting the shoreline for the day. But just then, as if rushing to John's aid, three smallmouth bass returned to feed, chasing after minnows into the shallows and gobbling up all they could. Whether they were the same three bass that he had spied earlier John could not say for sure. He was relieved, however, to ascertain that not one of them had the bright yellow stripes of the previous day's chatty visitor. He then started to think about how he might identify the individual bass, and even how he might possibly sex the fish when he remembered that he was not alone in his observations now. The redheaded girl was standing next to him. He promptly discontinued his bass-based train of thought and focused his energy on conversation.

"See? Aren't they neat?" John immediately thought he could have said something perhaps more eloquent, but felt satisfied enough with his observation.

"They sure are. I didn't know the big ones came so close in to shore."

"Neither did I. I guess that's what started me thinking."

"I hear ya. I guess that could get me goin', too." John was no longer sticking to his earlier opinion that he would stay by the water and study the fish no matter what the circumstances. He wanted to go wherever this girl went, whatever her name was.

The two of them stayed for another two passes from the fish, and then the redheaded girl had seen all she wanted to see for now. "I'm going to head back," she said.

"Okay, I'll come with you. They're just fish, anyway."

"Yeah, they are. But they're cool fish."

"Yes they are cool. But they'll be cool tomorrow, too. So let's go."

The two walked back up the road to the main camp, John still content to not know and ask the name of his new companion. It wouldn't be for several meetings by the lake that the subject of Gretchen's given name would come up.

It was almost a week after their initial encounter, and Gretchen was now helping John keep track of bass visits by recording the exact times of the sightings along with water visibility on a yellow legal pad. John was intently focused on his own pad, tracking feeding intervals, weather variations, and other data. John was in full fish swing this afternoon, and had practically forgotten the incident with the talking fish. He chatted enthusiastically about how the task at hand was now a group function and that he would have to adjust his projections for the number of trips he would need to make to the outhouse. He might have gone on at even greater length, factoring in the probable number of times the outhouse would be closed for maintenance, when Gretchen broached the subject of John not ever saying her name.

"You don't even know what my name is," said Gretchen, after recording the day's water visibility condition.

"That's not true. Of course I know your name."

"Okay, then what is it? I only told you twenty times."

"Your name? It's er... it's—"

"You don't know it." Gretchen understood that John was a different sort of boy, but this pushed her to the limits of her compassion.

Sensing his companion's dismay, he tried to make light of the situation. "What's so important about names, anyway? Especially since we're doing important research here."

Gretchen crossed her arms and gave him a long-faced, stern look of disapproval. When it looked like she was about to cry, John knew he had no choice but to confess the truth.

"I can't remember names," he said, dropping his hands to his sides, the right holding the pencil, the left gripping the pad.

"What?"

"I can't remember names. Ever since my accident, I can't remember anyone's name. And I'm not so good with instructions, either. Sometimes I'm a little better with instructions, but that comes and goes."

"You're serious?"

"If I was joking it wouldn't be very funny, now would it?"

"No, I guess not." There was a momentary silence. "My name is Gretchen."

"That's a pretty name." John paused for a second. "I really wish I could remember it," he said, ingenuously.

"That's one of the nicest and strangest things anyone's ever said to me."

John began to blush.

"Hey, quit turning your face red. And why don't you write my name down on your pad. At least while you have the pad you'll be able to remember my name."

"I'll probably forget I wrote it on the pad."

"I'll remind you."

"You will?"

"Yes, I will." Gretchen took John's pad, wrote her name in capital letters across the top, handed John's pad back to him, and gave him a delicate kiss on the cheek. John blushed as if instantly sunburnt.

"C'mon! You're face is almost as red as my hair."

"I'm not trying to make my face red, really I'm not, er—" John was already struggling for her name. Gretchen pointed to where she had written at the top of the pad.

"—Gretchen," said John, almost proudly.

"You're so cute," she said.

John put his hand over his face as if he could wipe away its rubicund state. She pulled his hand away from his face and kissed his cheek again. John's eyes rolled with embarrassment and delight, and would have continued doing so if they weren't frozen by movement on the periphery of his vision.

"Hey look!" he said. "Four bass—there's a new one!"

Gretchen turned her face to the shallows.

"Oh wow. Will you look at that—what are we going to do now, John?" The two youths stood for a moment watching the four fish pursue a zigzag chase of a school of minnows. All this commotion had not gone unnoticed in the lake habitat itself, and all at once a northern pike over three feet long appeared to shred the water, its mouth snapping quickly and everywhere. Its tail slapped the surface, the shallow water unable to contain its long green and yellow-spotted body in its frenzied feeding maneuvers. In a moment it was all over, the water turbid, obscuring the results of the fracas.

John scratched his chin a moment before speaking, rubbing his thumb in an unthinking circular motion up against his yellow pad, and peering almost blankly into the churning murk.

"We're gonna need bigger pads," he said.

4

YOU HAVE THAT FAMILIAR
FISH-FACE LOOK

◑

THOUGH JOHN AND GRETCHEN's yellow pad size ultimately remained the same, time did pass quickly as it is wont to do. Summer ended, and the two youths parted. They promised to stay in touch, but never did as such promises go. But a bond had been forged, and although distance and the vagaries of youth caused them to drift apart, they would never really lose one another for as long as they lived. Even if their paths were never to cross again, each of them had left on each other an irreducible impression, one which would never be forgotten—which for John was no small accomplishment.

As it turned out, they would not have to wait a lifetime or anything close to be reunited. Twelve years later, in the early winter of 1984, John was working in a pet store in lower Manhattan, having moved to New York City during the previous year. There, he worked as an inventory clerk, being pressed into sales when required. He wasn't the world's greatest salesman, but people seemed to warm enough to the peculiar way about him and his novel utilization of his time-honored life accessory, the yellow legal pad.

"Can I help you, miss?" he asked an attractive red-haired woman in a red and black plaid scarf and tan knockoff Burberry gabardine winter trench coat, strolling the aisles and peering through the small rectangular windows of the tanks into the various fishy worlds. Something beyond her pleasing looks drew John to her, whether It was the way she drew apparent delight with each new aquatic vista upon which she landed or just the general, assured but not officious way in which she carried herself. Quickly processing all this information led John to the tentative conclusion that the woman looked like someone he knew. But then so many people looked familiar to John whom he could not place exactly that he tended to dismiss the feeling until informed otherwise.

"Oh, I'm just looking. Killing time, actually. I don't know why, but something about looking at fish does something for me."

"Gee, I know what you mean. I wish we could just keep 'em all, to be honest with you. I'd put 'em all in one giant communal tank to best simulate their natural environment."

"That would be novel for a pet store."

"It sure would. Especially if we didn't sell the fish. Actually, I haven't figured that part out yet. Yeah and so speaking of sales, which is what I'm obliged to do, we're having a special on neon tetras. And to be honest with you, they really are excellent neon tetras as far as the species goes. And I say that with full disclosure that neon tetras are not anything like my favorite fish."

"Neon tetras? I thought they were a punk rock group."

"Those are the—" John looked on the clipboard he was carrying for reference. "—*Bush* Tetras. Actually, because of them we've seen an unprecedented upsurge in neon tetra sales, regardless of the quality of the specimens. We even play the Bush Tetras single in the store every two hours, though to me every time I hear the song it sounds new to me."

Something about the salesperson's tone and mannerisms was familiar. "Do I know you?" asked the young woman.

"I don't think so. But I have a hard time remembering most people I meet."

"Like you can't remember their name?" The young woman smiled.

"Actually, yes. Wait—who are you?" John took a quick and direct glimpse into his prospective customer's green eyes before shyly turning away.

"Let me jog your memory," she said, and kissed him gently on the cheek, whispering "Do you have any smallmouth bass for sale?"

John stood there, frozen, now staring at Gretchen with his mouth agape.

"Yep, it's you," she said.

"Gr... Gr... " John struggled with a fusillade of memories, feelings, and most of all with the name of the woman with whom he was talking. She took the legal pad and pen from John and wrote her name in capital letters across the top of the page. John read the name and then flung his arms out, legal pad in one hand and pen in the other.

"Gretchen—oh my god!"

"How've you been, fish boy?"

They embraced, nearly leaping into each other's arms.

"It's so-o-o good to see you," he said. John's eyes were closed and he breathed in her scent as he pressed his face to the side of her head. He had hugged her before she got on the bus that was to take her back home after camp twelve years ago. He reeled in the sensory memory of her essence, and held her as if to crush all time between that last hug and the present moment.

"It *is* so good to see you, too. But John... "

"Yes?"

"You're sticking your pen in my back."

John released his hug and took a step back all in one motion. "I'm so sorry!"

"Don't worry about it. It's almost appropriate."

"Jeez, really. I haven't seen you in like a dozen years and practically the first thing I do is stab you. Let me make it up to you. Let me buy you lunch."

"Well... okay. But just a cup of coffee for now."

"Sure. It's my lunch break in five minutes. I can tell because the kissing gouramis are at the surface of their tank and expecting food. Look." John pointed to a tank just a few feet away where the oval-shaped white fish John had mentioned were expectantly cruising just below the surface, their mouths opening and closing in an apparent practice run of their lunchtime drill. "Let me feed them. I'll get my coat, and then I'll be right with you."

"I'll wait outside. I wouldn't want to be the reason your gouramis missed out on lunch. If they don't eat they won't have strength for kissing the rest of the day." She winked at John, who smiled back, watching her leave before going to fetch the appropriate flakes.

John and Gretchen sat by the window at a coffee shop around the corner from the pet store. A sidewalk vendor had already set up a stock of over a hundred Christmas trees for sale, though it was still too early in December for the man to be doing much business, especially early in the work week. Watching the man tidy the display of his merchandise for lack of commerce, Gretchen filled John in on the details of her life in New York. Though they hadn't spoken in a dozen years, it only took a few minutes to fall back into the comfortable—if idiosyncratic—conversational pattern of their pre-teen association.

"So you're working a big time P.R. job," he said, taking a sip of his cappuccino. "That's great. One of my roommates went to NYU, too. He majored in Chinese."

"Chinese language or Chinese history?"

"Good question. All I know is that he orders in Chinese food and then tries to start a conversation with the delivery guy." Gretchen thought briefly of questioning the logic of John's response, but then remembered that this was John talking. She changed the subject. "And so how did you get to be in New York, Mr. Keller?"

"Oh, I started going with this girl for a few months back home. Then she wanted to come to New York, and for me to come with her. It was getting kinda boring at the Feed 'N' Seed where I worked in Garfield Heights, anyway. I'm just not that into grain, you know?"

"Oh yeah. People say grain is exciting, but personally I just don't get it."

"Hey, it's not altogether boring, and the farmers are nice enough, I guess. But when this girl—"

"What's her name?" Gretchen immediately wished she could rescind her request. But John was prepared, leafing through his notebook calendar and finding her name on an interior page.

"Her name was...Gwendolyn. You taught me this trick when we were at camp: write down the pretty girl's name."

"Oh stop." It was Gretchen's turn to move her eyes away, however slightly.

"I'm just gonna keep going here. So when—" John had to go to his notebook for reference. "—*Gwendolyn* asked me if I wanted to come with her to New York City, I said sure, why not? We got along well enough, though we probably should've tried living together first. I'm just not your run-of-the-mill boyfriend, you know."

"What did you do? This isn't going to upset me, is it?"

"No, I was just being me. She threw me out because I kept a running count of the number of articles of clothing she owned."

"Okay. That's unsettling."

"Yes and no. I was very open about it. She could never understand that it had nothing to do with keeping track of how much money she spent, or that she had to worry that she was going to wake up one morning and find me and all of her clothes gone."

"There's a reassuring statement."

"I know!"

John had missed the irony in Gretchen's response. But the ingenuousness of John's ensuing reaction reminded Gretchen of her childhood attraction for this man. No matter how offbeat his reasoning, he was right there in front of you all the time, pathologically incapable of anything more than the smallest lie or manipulation. She now just wanted to hear him talk. She was now fully conscious that listening to his screwball reasoning was something she had missed all these years.

"It was purely a mental exercise that helped me maintain my bearing in the relationship." This was true. John played this particular mind game to keep his equilibrium as best as he could living in a strange town, carrying maps and atlases everywhere he went. "I even told her I could probably stop counting the clothes, but then I'd probably end up enumerating and categorizing something else. I did try the pots and pans, but there just wasn't enough of them—and hardly ever a change in quantity to make it interesting." There was a brief pause as they stared out through the window onto the street, each taking a sip of their coffee.

"You're a walk on the weird side, Keller."

"I know."

"And so what are you doing for dinner on Thursday?" Gretchen asked.

John pulled out his yellow pad from the backpack which he had brought with him. He flipped through the first few pages. "Thursday? Let's see... " Beneath sheets detailing the current population and health of every specimen in the pet store, John had reached his calendar section where the current day and month was written across the top of the first page, with successive pages detailing ensuing days. On each page was written the agenda for that day. In the evening, before going to bed, John would rip out the first page and put it in a shoe box marked "USED DAYS," in the event that he needed to reference some past specific. He thumbed ahead three days to the page marked "THURSDAY, DECEMBER 3rd," and reviewed his schedule for that day.

"Okay, this Thursday...let's see. It looks like I have another office temp job lined up—"

"I thought you worked in the pet store."

"That's only part-time, but I may get put on full-time soon. The manager really likes the way I keep track of things. But he's also concerned that I get too caught up in unnecessary details. The manager at the Feed 'N' Seed said the same thing. But that's all right—the pay isn't so great at the store, so it's better I keep my options open.

"You can do better than a pet store, John." Gretchen smiled.

"Yeah I know. But I have to admit that working there three days a week helps satisfy my curiosity. Right now I'm keeping tabs on the average water temperature of all the fish tanks. I gotta make sure there is consistency."

"You don't want to let that sort of thing get out of hand."

"You're making fun of me."

"I always made fun of you. You used to like it."

"As far as I can remember, I think I did. There's really been no one else I could talk to candidly about this stuff, other than a couple of therapists. And my last therapist fired me. Said he couldn't make sense of the superfluous details."

"But so much of everybody is superfluous details."

"Yeah, but he said I was all superfluous details. He said if there was some sort of 'inner me' then there was no way of reaching it behind a heavy shroud of tangentially relevant information."

"Sheesh. You should have fired him first."

"I was going to. It was pretty much a mutual decision. I always got the feeling that he found me incomprehensible, which is not a formal diagnosis you can send in to the shrink's society or whatever. Mostly, though, I think I just bored him."

"'Boring' is not the term I'd use to describe you. I can think of many others far more accurate."

"Well thanks, I think. Say, I gotta get back to work. Um, where do you want to meet for dinner?" John looked at his watch, and then handed the pad along with a pen to Gretchen, open to the coming Thursday's page.

"Why don't I just make you dinner at my place? You're not a serial killer, are you?"

"Not to my knowledge. But you can check the pad to see if I made any notes to the contrary."

"That's okay—I'll trust you." It wasn't like Gretchen to be incautious, inviting men she did not know well to come to her apartment. But even though she did not have great experience with the adult version of the boy with whom she spent the great part of one youthful summer, she felt uncommonly at ease with him from the moment she recognized who he was.

She looked at the pad and pen in her hands. "And other than checking for details on your latest killing spree, what would you like me to do with these?"

"Well, since we're meeting at your place, and so as to reduce the chances of my not being able to locate you, I'd really appreciate if you wrote down your address, phone number—"

"Of course, John, how else would I expect you to find—"

"—nearest cross streets, closest Subway line and appropriate stop, and any nearby significant landmarks."

"You don't need my Social Security number?"

"Why would I need that—?" John caught the joke this time. "Maybe next time," he said with a slight smile. "What time should I come over?"

"Seven is good," she replied as she filled up the bottom third of John's Thursday page with the requested information. John took back the pad, reviewed the details, and then took a quick look at his watch.

"Crap—it's 2:10 already. I'm going to be late turning down the heater in the iguana habitat."

"And you need to do that because...?"

"I'm trying to simulate the natural arc of the sun for them," John said, standing up and putting on his coat.

"And does this make the iguanas feel any better?" Gretchen stood as well, picking up the check that the waiter had left on the table.

"It's hard to tell," said John, putting down a five dollar bill to cover his cappuccino and croissant roll lunch. "Gauging iguana response isn't easy. They're a stoic bunch."

"That's the trouble with iguanas," said Gretchen with a smile.

"Oh you don't know the half of it," said John, playing along. "Hey, I'll see you Thursday." John gave a hurried wave goodbye and headed out the door. Gretchen watched him hurry out of sight, and then gathered her things to move along with the rest of the day.

5

TRASH
TALK

◑

THURSDAY CAME AND JOHN delivered himself promptly to his temp job at 8am. This was his third time working at the world corporate headquarters of Rug Nation, Inc., the world's leading carpet manufacturer, located in midtown Manhattan on the sixteenth floor at 9 West 57th Street. Most everyone who worked at Rug Nation referred to the company as "Rugnacious," even though management had several times sent out a memo warning that anyone found using that term would lose their year-end bonus rug of choice. They had sent one out the last time John had worked there, and upon reading the memo, John had thought he would be a lock to get an end-of-the-year rug, as it was enough of a chore remembering the proper name of his workplace, no less some derogatory alias.

John worked at Rug Nation in a variety of capacities. The task which suited him best was taking messages for executives to whom he was never introduced, filling in as needed for secretaries and assistants to those executives as needed. The fact that no one with an office at Rug Nation ever took a direct call was no doubt a catalyst for the spread of the Rugnacious epithet. For his stints in message processing, John was given a script printed on each card in a stack of 4x6 index cards from which he would read to callers: "I'm sorry but Mr. Farkle is not available at the moment. Can I take a message?" The name of the individual for whom he was currently working was handwritten in a space between "but" and "is." John would then write the message below the script on the card. If the person phoning wanted to converse further, John resorted to one of the ancillary responses provided at the bottom of the card. "You'll have to talk to Mr. Farkle." "He should be back very soon." "I'm not authorized to comment on such matters." Once the call was finished, he would then file the card in a tray marked "TAKEN," and wait for the next call.

Once an hour, an all but silent, humorless, and nameless young woman in severe, conservative office attire and horn-rimmed glasses, would collect John's messages from the tray, along with those from other temps working in the same capacity. It was the consensus among message takers that this card collector was an arbiter of what was and what was not needed to be passed on to their ultimate recipient, with the vast majority of messages never getting past her station. Judging from her demeanor and attire, it was further surmised that when she performed this task she did so in a basement office with access to an incinerator. There it was supposed that she derived immense pleasure from burning the messages one by one, throwing off her glasses and cackling hideously as she tossed message after message into the fire: "And you thought you were going to get a hold of the VP of Purchasing? Not while my blood still flows—HAHAHA!"

John probably would have eased in and out of this day without incident if he could have gone on working in message processing. At least there he had a script, a reference with which to guide him. But the message pool was full with regular staffers, and so John was put to work elsewhere. He was assigned to "General Assistance," which required him to perform on-the-spot tasks for whoever needed him at that moment.

John's time spent in General Assistance tested his mettle most severely. The previous time he worked "G.A.," as it was called, he had been assigned to lightly clean offices and workstations of those individuals absent or out of the office for the day. John's interpretation of light cleaning was to rearrange papers and personal effects in those spaces in a way that conformed to his vision of an optimal personal workflow. Upon returning to the office the following day, all seven individuals complained to the effect of "some asshole had moved their shit around and now they couldn't find anything." John was reprimanded, but given another chance in that all seven spaces were made otherwise spotless.

Earlier in the afternoon he had filed a set of documents according to a schema known only to him, a schema which he promptly forgot when questioned about it. Fortunately for John, the executive figured out what John had done and found the reorganization by date and degree of physical wear on each letter to be largely acceptable.

But now John had met his Waterloo. He stood paralyzed in the main lobby, carrying a can full of trash without a clue as to what to do with it. He struggled to remember what he had been instructed to do with the trash, and who had engaged him to do whatever it was he was supposed to do. A crowd began to gather. Persons passing back and forth from the elevators—and one woman waiting to go in for an appointment—reached out to him, offering assistance to the hapless John. With each offer of assistance, John looked more and more unfamiliar with the natural workings of the muscles in his body, evoking in those that encountered him something between pity and compassion.

Dave Hopkins and Dave Tompkins, two veteran employees from payroll and virtually indistinguishable from each other's poorly nourished selves in their wrinkled white shirts and chinos, began to hover about John and the trashcan like a workaday Greek chorus, expounding on his predicament. The Daves were as excited as the Daves could be, solemnly ecstatic to be doing something for entertainment other than redirecting persons looking for one Dave to the other Dave, explaining "You're looking for Dave *Hopkins*—I'm Dave Tompkins," and vice versa; before the second Dave would then send that person back to the first, and so on.

"Looks like regular trash to me. Why just don't you just chuck it?" said Dave Hopkins.

"He can't just chuck it—maybe someone wanted it shredded," answered Dave Tompkins, bobbing his head slightly. John tried to recall anything said to him about shredding, but all that came to mind were the different sizes and flavoring of shredded wheat cereal whose relative popularity he was tracking at his local grocer.

"I can hear soda cans in there. You don't shred soda cans," said Hopkins.

"Maybe he was supposed to remove them first and then shred the rest," answered Tompkins.

"Was there a memo today to that effect?"

"No memo," said Tompkins, "just a hunch."

"Hmm. This is getting complicated. Somebody should call somebody."

"But what good would that do? No one who has the power to do anything ever answers the phone at Rugnacious."

"Oh dear," thought John, exasperated, and the Daves buzzing around him wasn't making things any easier. He finally closed his eyes and summoned the image of the red-headed girl from his childhood that reappeared in the pet store a few days earlier. Although he knew it was a futile effort, he dedicated all his mental energy to trying to remember her name. "If there was one person in my life whom I'd like to be able to hail at will," he thought, "I really think it would be her."

John's deep dive into the inner recesses of his naming capacity and the Daves' impromptu symposium on the existential nature of John's garbage might have continued if Peg McElroy, the head of Human Resources did not appear from a door behind the receptionist to rescue John.

As head of Human Resources and thriving on efficiency, Peg was an energetic lifer at Rug Nation, having worked there exclusively since graduating from Bennington. Just under five feet and given to wearing knee-high one piece dresses in a predictable range of pastel shades, she was certainly not unattractive in her close-cropped brunette hairstyle, unfailingly sunny persona, and pleasing figure. But to Peg, a relationship presented too many human relations issues that could not be resolved with a memo, so she remained unattached in her early forties.

Now faced with an issue no memo could possibly make right, Peg rushed to John's side—albeit in a very controlled rush.

"I hope he wasn't bothering you," Peg remarked, with a forced smile for the Daves and those standing by watching the drama unfold.

"A most curious situation. Unexpected food for thought," said Hopkins.

"Have you an answer to the riddle of the trash?" followed Tompkins, quickly.

"It's my trash," said Peg McElroy. "He was just supposed to empty it."

"Aha. Then no shredding was called for," said Hopkins.

"No. I apologize if this situation has inconvenienced any of you in any way."

"Not at all. 'Twas a welcome diversion. I'm more disappointed that my hunch was wrong," said Tompkins, almost sadly.

The Daves broke their holding pattern and went off together, in step, to return to their payroll chambers on the other side of the office. They gestured in their follow-up discussion to the incident, looking synchronized in their retreat. The last few hangers-on went about their business as well.

And with that, Peg McElroy grabbed John's free arm and ushered him back through the door behind the receptionist into the main inner office.

Once inside her office and standing in front of her desk, she took a moment to collect herself, took a deep sigh, and addressed the now forlorn John.

"What is wrong with you, John? I ask you to simply take my trash and empty it in the garbage can in the kitchen, and you wind up creating a scene in the lobby."

John tottered back and forth on his heels near the back wall of Peg's office, still clutching the garbage can like a security blanket. He tried to draw on a comparable incident in his life—or in the biography of any one else who might come to mind—but he could find none to draw upon to ameliorate his current situation.

"Just give me that," demanded Peg, quietly.

"Just give you what?" asked John.

"The trashcan."

For a moment, John was baffled. He then realized he was still holding the bin in his arms.

"Oh—yes, here!" John thrust the container in Peg's direction with such nervous enthusiasm that the topmost trash spilled out onto the floor like fresh popcorn jumping out of the hopper.

"I'll pick it up, don't you worry." He handed the receptacle to Peg and squatted to pick up the crumpled pieces of paper and other detritus scattered about the carpet.

Now holding the trashcan, Peg sighed once more before addressing John, who was now under the desk with his legs sticking out, retrieving not only the scattered waste but whatever else there had escaped the cleaning company's best vacuuming efforts.

"Look, John, you're a really nice kid, and I didn't think anyone could screw up emptying a waste basket. But I was wrong. I'm sorry, but I'm going to have to let you go."

"I'll be up in a second, Ms. McElroy. You wouldn't believe the junk under here," said John, completing his sentence as he stood, hands full of ancient memos, a few paper clips, and a tiny red leather change purse.

"I'll bet you've been looking for this for a while," he said, handing her the empty purse.

"Actually I have. Thank you." She put the purse on her desk.

"Glad to be of service. Um, did you say something when I was under the desk? I couldn't quite hear."

"Yes I did. I'm going to have to let you go."

John immediately protested. "Just give me one more chance, ma'am, please. The people in message processing say no one can take a message like I can."

"I know, but I can't risk another incident like the one out there just now. It doesn't look good for the company. I'll let the agency know if we'll be needing your services in the future."

"Yes, Ms. McElroy. I'm sorry to have been of trouble."

John trundled out of her office and to make his way home.

Peg McElroy had a small flask of bourbon in the furthest recess of her desk's bottom drawer. Someone had given it to her as a gag gift at the office Christmas party three years ago, as Peg had worked hard to craft her image as the steady, sober, no-nonsense mastermind of the Rug Nation workforce. Having all but forgotten the bottle until now, she quietly retrieved it from the drawer, as if she were taking out an old document to review.

Once in hand, however, such composure went out the window as she ripped off the bottle cap and downed almost a third of the stuff in one gulp. Done with her initial swig, she took another hefty swallow, and then several more until she had emptied almost two thirds of the bottle. With her mind sufficiently benumbed and her body unaccustomed to liquor of any quantity, Peg deflated into the core of her leather chair and closed her eyes. Feeling the effects like the sinking of an ocean liner, she dangled her left hand over the arm of her seat and let the bottle drop to the floor, remaining conscious only long enough to make sure the flask was standing upright on the plastic floor protector under the wheels of her chair.

6

TRAIN
OF THOUGHT

◑

JOHN RODE THE SUBWAY home that day desperately trying to retrace his steps and determine how and why he lost his way with the wastebasket. He could get as far as the hallway with the giant stuffed billfish on the wall, at which point he made a left. But after that he drew a blank.

Billfish and then blank
Billfish and then blank
Billfish and then blank

The sequence played over and over and over in his mind, with John hoping to come up with a different result so that the next time he could get it right. But each time he ran it through, the blank remained blank. Finally, John slumped back in his subway car seat and drooped his head, looking at the empty seat next to him. In doing so he took notice of a *Byte* magazine left behind on the seat.

Byte was the leading consumer magazine focusing on the nascent field of computer graphics for personal and business use. Though John had no knowledge of computer graphics whatsoever, he sensed something different, something compelling about this publication. A sense of curiosity and awe overcame him as if he might be handling some valuable relic. He opened the magazine to an article about how to most efficiently download a certain font to one's laser printer. John read the article in full, comprehending only a tiny portion of it.

"Fonts. Download times. Megabits and megabytes. Heavy stuff." As he thought this to himself, John felt a vague pride that he had done his small part to keep his head in the game, a game for which there was no rulebook in the world that could help John make real sense of it.

But when he turned the page, what what was waiting there changed his life forever.

The image on the page—a simple pie chart—transported John to some other previously unexplored, cerebral dimension. There was no explanation for the hypnotic effect, only that the page seemed to him to glow like the control room computer banks in some 50's heavily saturated Technicolor scifi flick. Completely transfixed, he skipped his stop where he normally switched to the downtown local train. And his obliviousness didn't end with missed subway connections. He completely ignored being panhandled and—more significantly—failed to register the beggar's body odor which had everyone else in the car covering their face and gagging. An overstressed new mother running over John's feet with a stroller carrying her three-month-old howling baby, along with the cursory apology issued, went completely unnoticed. And finally, John took no account of being whacked soundly on his shin with an umbrella by an elderly woman for not moving his legs out of her path to the door when the train came to her stop.

All of the above was completely lost on John, for now, having transgressed the the initial allure of the colors of the photos in the magazine, he was now riveted to an article about a program called Lotus 1-2-3, an early spreadsheet program. John couldn't and didn't understand why he found this so fascinating. He just did. All that mattered was that a door had been opened and he had walked through it. It was not until he was well through this new door of his consciousness and settled into an overstuffed chair in its living room that he heard a voice calling him back to the tactile world, a pronouncement which something inside of him knew could not be ignored.

"Hey buddy, if you plan on spending the night, there's a motel about three blocks from here." Standing directly over John with his hands at his sides, the conductor and his tongue-in-cheek suggestion finally burst his reverie's bubble.

"Uh, no, I wasn't. Why do you ask?"

"Because we're at Coney Island—last stop. And we've been sittin' here for ten minutes. This train is goin' in for service so you're gonna have to get off. I know this is a nice spot, but the price of a subway token doesn't cover lodging."

"Oh wow. Guess I spaced out." John craned his neck to inspect the seaside twilight. "I'll be going then. I have to get back to Manhattan."

"Then there's your ride back sittin' on the opposite track. I suggest you come back in the summer. It's a lot nicer then."

"Oh yeah. Sure." John collected his things, being certain not to leave the magazine on the train, and crossed the platform for the inbound "F" train, still in a trance. The only thing that caught his attention, and so vaguely that he was unaware that he was thinking about it, was that as he waited for the trip to begin he looked out at the Ferris Wheel, and saw it as a gigantic pie chart too crudely and dimly drawn to readily communicate any perceptible ratio.

Ninety minutes later John made it back to his lower Manhattan apartment. He tried the key, missing the insertion point in the door lock several times by a wide margin in rapid succession, his adrenalin rushing from consuming the information, ratios and color schemes now buzzing inside him. A thousand questions jumbled like popcorn popping in his mind—questions for the author of the magazine article, the creator of the software, the publisher of the magazine, the newsstand vendor of the magazine, the driver who delivered the magazine to the newsstand—anyone who was even remotely associated with the publication. When he did manage to place the key in the lock, he more fell than walked through the door into the communal living room.

One of his roommates, the perpetually unemployed Tim Zeeman, stood in the common room in his white underwear top and bottom and socks, drinking a Pabst Blue Ribbon and watching a fuzzy reception of a soccer game on the house seven-inch black and white TV. He was always glad to see John. It gave him something to do.

"Hey, my man Johnny! Qué pasa? Good to see you, pal. I thought maybe you forgot your way home from Rugnacious, ran into a shag. Ran into a *shag*, get it? Shag carpet?"

"I get it."

"Hey, I was gettin' worried. Almost ready to send out a search party, bro. Hey, where's the free rug you said you were gonna bring back?"

"I never said that. You said that."

"Well that sucks, man. I need a new rug. Can't get the beer stink out of the one I got."

"Sorry to hear."

Tim shook his head in disappointment, sending a chain reaction down to his gut, which shook correspondingly. Tim's paunch was already firmly established, though nowhere near the exercise in exponential growth it would demonstrate in later years.

John was holding the magazine closely to his coat, as if it was some sort of contraband.

"Say, what you got there, dude?"

"A magazine."

"Well I can see that, and I can see that it's too big to be a *TV Guide*, which is most unfortunate as I am so in the dark when it comes to much of the upcoming programming, dude. I mean, if you don't know the College Football Bowl schedule, then what do you know?"

"I don't follow college football."

"Well there you go, there you go. You can see it all over your face—the schedule is missing, man."

Tim's habit was to finish most of his declarations with an informal pronoun of some sort—"dude," "bro," "man," etc., as if he thought whatever he had said wouldn't make sense without them.

"So what've you got there, dude—porn? Can I see it then when you're done with it?"

"It's not porn."

John held the magazine out in front of him. The cover featured a young software inventor apparently standing on a giant-sized keyboard in front of a monolithic computer. John had actually been taken in by this photographic sleight of hand, and wondered where and how they could have built such a gigantic computer system.

"Man, you're right. That is definitely not porn." Tim snatched the magazine out of John's outstretched hands.

"Hey—give that back!"

"Cool your jets, bro. I'm not gonna start a bonfire with it or nothing. I just wanna look for a minute." Tim riffled through the pages. "Wow. I didn't know you were into shit like this. I don't really get it, and I had four years of college. Here—" Tim handed the magazine back to John, "—it's all yours. I'll stick to what I know."

What Tim knew amounted to a spotty knowledge of mid-nineteenth century Chinese politics that he had studied at NYU. What Tim did, specifically, was to trot out his questionable knowledge of Chinese history to every Chinese food deliveryman who came to the door. "That Qing dynasty, man, they really blew it. Those asshole warlords just couldn't get their shit together to save their own butts, y'know what I mean, dude?" Tim's invitation to discuss Chinese history with deliverymen would inevitably be met with a polite but confused smile, and most often interpreted as a request to repeat the sum total of the bill.

John took the *Byte* magazine and went into his room. He shut the door, lay down on his bed, and set the magazine flat upon his chest. He closed his eyes and let the afterglow of the afternoon's events swirl about his conscience, and with clasped hands pressed the magical presence of the magazine closer to his chest. The urge to further delve into the magazine would have no doubt overtaken him if he hadn't become aware of the string attached to his left index finger, which he knew referred to some imminent event or another in his life. Upon lifting his hand, he noted that it was a yellow piece of string, which indicated that he should check his yellow schedule pad for further instruction. Retrieving the pad from his wooden night table and reviewing the schedule, he was reminded that he was expected at Gretchen's in an hour. Lifting himself off the bed, he placed the magazine on his night table and then set the yellow string on top of the periodical, so he would not forget to bring the magazine with him to dinner.

7
SOMEWHERE THERE'S
A CHART FOR US

◑

J OHN ARRIVED LATE FOR dinner at Gretchen's apartment, where he was anxious to discuss the afternoon's epiphany. Gretchen had put out candles, and bought a bottle of her favorite Cabernet. On the table she set out matched china sporting the branding of a defunct hotel in Minneapolis, a collection which she had picked up at a flea market over the summer. She knew it was a long shot that John would appreciate her setting the mood in her tiny second floor studio apartment this way, but she could in no way have predicted that this evening she would be discussing by candlelight as unlikely a topic as computer graphics. By the time they had finished the roast chicken dinner and were sipping espresso, Gretchen was still hanging with John's passion for the subject, although that ability was approaching its limit. "So you plug figures into a program, and then you press a button and the results are displayed in a chart. That's what you're talking about, right?"

"Yes. That's it—that's it exactly. Do you want to see the magazine again?"

"No no—that's quite all right. I got it. I think there's a guy in the back somewhere at work that does that kind of thing."

"Really? Do you think I could come watch him?"

"Um, yeah, I guess. I don't see why not, except that I've never actually heard the guy talk. I don't really know if he communicates by conventional means with other people in the office. I'd have to ask someone—"

John shifted abruptly in his chair. "Would you do that for me? That would be just terrific."

"Sure, I mean, why not? But I can't promise anything." Gretchen moved her chair closer to John. "But you're going to have to do one thing for me in return."

"What's that?"

"That we don't talk about pie charts or computer graphics or anything like that for a while."

"So what do you wanna talk about—iguanas? That would be fine, I guess. I can talk iguanas any time of the day. But the graphics stuff is like *life-changing.*"

Gretchen, smiled, dipped and shook her head. She put up her left hand, palm out, waving it slightly in front of her face.

"I don't care right now," she said, looking right into his eyes.

John began to protest before being mesmerized by her gaze. The hand with which she had shown John gentle disapprobation now stroked the hair on side of his head, moving down to touch his cheek. She then brought her face closer to his. John flinched nervously, moving back a few inches in his seat.

"Wh-what are you doing?" he said.

"What do you think I'm doing?"

"I think you are initiating a romantic moment," he said.

"That's an excellent guess."

"I have to warn you that I'm not very skilled at this type of activity."

"And I guessed that."

"The woman I came to New York with said she might have overlooked my counting her clothes if I'd paid more attention during romantic interludes."

"Maybe her clothes were more interesting than she was."

John scratched his chin, nodding. "That could be."

Gretchen stroked the side of his head once more. "I'm willing to bet on it."

"Really? What sort of odds would you take—"

Gretchen cut off John's gambling contemplation with a kiss on the lips. As they kissed, John scrambled to maintain his equilibrium by calculating the odds of two sets of lips randomly meeting on a New York City street as Gretchen's and his were now. Before he could figure beyond an educated guess of slim-to-none, she pulled her lips from his.

"And so how was that? Were you thinking about my clothes?"

"Not at all."

"Do you want to do it again?"

"Sure." John was encouraged that she hadn't asked about what he was actually thinking, and was forced to admit to himself that he was experiencing elation unlike he'd ever known or could have predicted in any sort of calculation he had employed in his life until this point. So they kissed again, this time with more romantic fervor as Gretchen put her arms around John, a move which John awkwardly echoed. As he fumbled without success to find a natural place for his hands on Gretchen's torso, he found it more and more difficult to focus on the non-phenomenon of random public lip junctures and whatever else he could think of to keep his cognitive balance.

Gretchen stared into John's essentially present eyes as their mouths separated. "You're a pretty good kisser. I'm surprised."

"Thank you. It helped that I thought of harpooning whales, which I had to cut short as I really can't stand the whole history of that operation. Hey, did you see 'Star Trek: The Voyage Home,' the one about the whales? That was an excellent film—"

"Shut up. I can't believe you're thinking about harpooning whales and Star Trek while I'm kissing you."

"Hey, it worked, didn't it?"

Gretchen's disgruntled countenance quickly turned to one of bemused agreement. "Well yeah. And what are you thinking about now?" Gretchen took his right hand in hers and placed it on her left breast.

John's hand showed what appeared to be early signs of turning to stone. "I..."

"Come on. Tell me. What are you thinking about now, Mr. Male Sexuality? Hot air balloons? Jellyfish? Those Japanese goldfish with the big bug eyes?"

John was close to breaking into a sweat. "I was thinking..."

"Yes?"

" ...about the annual U.S. Jello consumption for the previous decade... "

"That's it?"

" ...and how lucky I am to have found you again."

Gretchen pressed his hand tighter to her chest, moving his hand over her nipple. John suppressed the impulse to calculate the relative size of the nipple itself in relation to the entire bosom, and simply let himself enjoy the sensation. "I knew there was a preferred reaction in you somewhere. It just needed a little help coming out."

"You were certain?"

"Not for sure. But I was hoping the shock would improve my chances."

Gretchen maintained her hold of John's hand, and led him over to the living room. They fell together onto the green pull-out couch, dragging down the beaded purple madras shawl covering the back of it with them. Trying to find a comfortable position for himself, John ended up taking the entire covering with him as he fell off the couch onto the floor. Lying on her side, Gretchen looked down at John, who was trying to right himself.

"Are you coming back up here?"

"Yes," said John, breathing heavily after wrestling himself free of the shawl.

"When?"

"Er, now, I guess." John leapt back up onto the couch and draped the shawl over the both of them. As John swooped up from the floor the draft he created with the fabric extinguished all of the candles except for one in the far corner of the room. That was all the illumination they would need for the next hour or so.

The lovers lay on the couch under the shawl, Gretchen holding John in her arms, his head comfortably resting on her breast. By this time the last candle had gone out, and they were lit only by the electric glow of the city night streaming in through the window. The sound of a car alarm going off down the block broke the near silence of their gentle breathing. John opened his eyes. Once the car alarm finally shut off, Gretchen spoke.

"You're not such a bad lover, Mr. Keller, once you get going. I thought I was going to be giving a lot more instruction."

"I haven't had much practice."

"We can work on that. And how many times have you made love?"

"Only a few times, that is at least as far as memory serves. But there might have been other such interactions. You'd have to check the pad."

"I'm not going to the pad on this one, thank you." She paused, and moved his head so she could look him in the eyes. "Do you like my body?"

John started to feel a bit squeamish. "Um, well yeah, I think you've got a great body, it's like out of a medical textbook—"

She gently put her finger to his lips. "There's no need to act like you're twelve years old. It's me you're talking to. I want an answer from John the adult." Gretchen took her finger away.

John stared up into the ceiling, breathing deeply and calmly. "It's the most beautiful thing I've ever seen," he said finally, without any trace of boyish, hyperactive enthusiasm.

Gretchen rolled on top of him, looked into his eyes, and all at once they were making love again, this time with one or two less conjugal stumbling blocks than their initial effort.

In the morning, they sat at the kitchen table, glowing with awareness of the wondrous threshold they had crossed the previous evening.

"I have a meeting early so I have to run. But thanks heavens it's Friday, because I have a great idea for the weekend," said Gretchen.

"What's that?" John said, taking a sip of his coffee.

"We can pull out the sleeper bed." She smiled, and John met her smile with a wet coffee kiss. They separated and grasped hands across the table.

"And so what are you going to do today, John?"

"I gotta work at the store ten to six. But before that I'm going to read the magazine some more. I don't know if I've done a good job explaining what's happened inside me as far as the graphics are concerned—hell, I don't think I really understand it myself. All I know is that something's clicked."

Gretchen gave her head a quick quarter turn. "Weird, Keller—very weird. But if it makes you happy, then chart away." She stood up and rummaged through her pocketbook, retrieving her set of keys from the bottom. "Hey, I'm going to leave you with my key. Be back here at six, or I'm going to beat you with a pie chart, do you hear?"

John was already engrossed in the magazine. "Yes, ma'am," he said, not lifting his eyes from the publication.

The ends of Gretchen's lips curled up ever so slightly, and she bent over and kissed him on the top of his head. "I really like you, John Keller."

"Yes ma'am," he said, again.

Gretchen placed the keys on the table and put on her coat. "Jeez," she thought, looking at John reading the magazine, "I just spent the most romantic evening of my life and he's already acting like it's a bad marriage and bored with me. Maybe I should rethink this." She turned for the door.

"Oh, and one more thing," said John as he got up from his chair.

"Yes?" said Gretchen, standing in the middle of the kitchen and watching John approach.

"Just this." John took her in his arms and dipped her halfway to the floor, where he bent over to whisper in her ear. "I really *really* like you too, you know?" He then took her mouth in his for one last soul-shaking kiss, pulsating and lasting more than a minute. "Have a good day at work," he said, raising her back to her original standing position, "and I'll see you tonight."

Mildly dazed but incomparably elated, Gretchen collected herself and eventually neatened her makeup in the mirror on the door. She gave John one more look, saw he was back ensconced in the periodical, smiled, and headed out.

Gretchen shut the door behind her gently, and John did not hear the latch turn at all. But even if John had been paying the closest attention to the events surrounding him, he would not been able to see or hear the two invisible entities standing in the kitchen by the table, eyeing him carefully.

"I don't unterstand vhy vee need zeh girl involved," said one of the spectral voices in a heavy German accent.

"It's going to help him evolve exactly to the place where we can use him best," said the other in a solemn, deep tone.

"Acch, he found zeh magazine—zat's all he needed. Vimmen? All zay are required for is zeh reproduction—"

"Shut up or I'll toss your essence out the window and have it impaled on the World Trade Center radio tower."

"You vouldn't do zat to me, vould you?

"Yes I 'vould.' With pleasure."

"But I sought vee verr good friends by now."

"You are one of the most heinous pieces of garbage known to creation for which I am willing to cut some slack at the moment as you currently serve my purposes. If that fits your definition of a good friend, then we are—oh, how do the kids put it these days? Ahh, yes—then we are B-F-F-F."

"B-F-F-F? Vot does zat mean?"

"Oh, I don't think there's an explanation that would make any sense to you."

"But—"

"But nothing. Forget about it. I've seen what I came to see and I am satisfied. It's only a few more years now. I'm ready to turn the situation over to the Transport Department, anyway. Our work is done for the time being. Let's go."

And even though there would never be any trace of their ever being there, they were there no more, returning again to whence they came.

8
CHATTER
AND CHARTS

◖

YEARS PASSED AND JOHN Keller's facility for presentation
graphics grew to the point where he became known in the
advertising trade as the person to call when it came to such
things. After taking a series of rewarding positions and gathering
considerable acclaim in the industry, he accepted a job at Hadfield &
Co., a leading advertising firm located in Midtown. There he processed
data and created charts and other graphics without peer. He was
well-compensated for his efforts, and he and Gretchen settled into a
comfortable lifestyle, moving into a loft space together in the Flatiron
District of lower Manhattan. Gretchen had enjoyed vocational success in
her own right, being named VP of Operations by the age of thirty-four
at Wellspring Partners publicity firm. She exploited her innate sense of
what made people tick and what motivated them to respond positively, a
talent her clients and employer much appreciated.

John's success came with no title, nor did he want one. His card read
"JOHN KELLER, CHARTS, ETC." He had no interest in climbing
any corporate ladder he might bump into or walk under. His past
experience as a temp worker and subsequent unsuccessful gigs had left
an indelible impression on him. He knew that he wanted nothing to
do with the mystifying and frequently cutthroat machinations of the
everyday corporate world. He lived for the uniquely itemized representa-
tion of everything and anything that crossed his path, but he hardly ever
had a thought for who might be ultimately viewing his work. John could
have been preparing charts and graphs for the President of the United
States or a troupe of chimpanzees—it mattered little which it was.

What did matter a great deal to John was the feeling that his position
was a tenuous one, and that today he might be considered the best at
what he did but that tomorrow someone might take his crown. So it was

with great eagerness that he woke before dawn in early 2003 to switch on his home desktop computer. Once the machine had powered up, he followed instructions Gretchen had written on his faithful yellow pad on how to log on to the Internet, a concept John had yet to fully grasp yet appreciated as it gave him access to unlimited data.

Motivating John to rise so early this morning was that leading graphics program developer Shuffling Mushroom Systems had just released its latest version of its flagship product, the Graphic Salad Creative Suite. John was anxious to pore through the details on the company website to see if the firm had done anything whatsoever to enhance or update the chart creation capabilities of the software. John read through the information with the eagerness of a dog about to receive a pre-packaged bacon treat.

Zip. Zilch. Nada. The big sombrero. A stark, belching, bubbling, sulphuric zero of resoundingly inconsequential proportions. Once again, Shuffling Mushroom had chosen to ignore the presentational sliver of the graphics spectrum, and John couldn't have been more pleased. In fact, he was so carried away with the news that he planted a huge, not altogether graceful, and to be honest, downright sloppy kiss on the center of his computer screen. So emphatic was John's lip lunge that he had to reel himself in to contain his excitement, nearly slapping himself in the face in the process. "Get a hold of yourself. You'd think you won a million bucks," he thought, lips still on glass.

With a small but definite "pop," John unglued himself from the screen, and straightened himself up in the pre-dawn crepuscule. While brushing off his shoulders—as if his shoulders had anything to do with his composure—he heard a matter-of-fact male voice speaking a few feet behind him.

"Hey, that was a pretty classy move you made with your computer screen there. But don't worry—I ain't gonna tell your girlfriend."

John whipped around in his chair, perhaps expecting to spy an intruder of some sort, only to find nothing out of the ordinary. The experience was not new to John. Ever since his accident he had heard voices on occasion, either on the periphery of sensation or in delusional form. Recognizing that it was a hallucination satisfied John as to why it appeared that a fish had told him that day by the lake that he needed to get working on his brain. Most times, he found himself being addressed in a Germanic accent. This voice was different, however. It sounded like a veteran used car salesman trying to be chummy.

Suspicious and agitated, John searched the living room for signs of a forced entry, but could find none. He checked the two windows on the north wall, and they were as firmly locked as when he had shut them the previous evening. He went to secure the rest of the apartment, with his first stop to check in on Gretchen in the bedroom. He leaned over her still sleeping form, and once he had determined that she was breathing regularly and had not been murdered in her sleep, he was able to take his anxiety down a half a notch. He now set about searching the bedroom for evidence of intrusion. He peered underneath the bed and found nothing but the instruction manual for his new printer which he was absolutely positive he had put elsewhere and for which he had been searching these last few weeks.

The next move was to attack the closet. Not really expecting to find anything, but owing to some hastily conceived notion of thoroughness, he went so far as to rummage through Gretchen's collection of hats, scarves, and other winter garments on the top shelf of the closet, finding nothing suspicious. A search behind each one of her lineup of childhood teddy bears on a shelf on the far wall proved equally unalarming. It was only when he crawled under the large blue Persian rug at the foot of the bed to check if the downstairs neighbor had sawed a trap door in the apartment floor did John finally rouse his sleeping girlfriend. Barely awake, she hardly knew what to make of the twisting, shifting lump beneath the floor covering.

"John, is that you?"

"Of course it's me."

"Why are you under the rug?"

"I'm making sure you're safe."

"From the rug?"

"No, of course not from the rug," he said poking his head out from underneath the floor covering and brushing the dust off his red plaid pajamas.

"That's good to know," Gretchen said, stretching her arms and yawning. She looked out through the door toward the dim light of the living room. She knew it was too early to be awake yet, or at least too early to follow John down one of his arcane behavioral highways.

"Okay. Have fun with the rug, but not too much," she said, flopping her head back down on her pillow and nuzzling into it as deeply as she could before closing her eyes. As Gretchen began to drift off, John clambered out from under the rug and stood at the foot of the bed, satisfied that the floor was secure.

"Did you hear any voices?" he said.

"Just yours," replied Gretchen, without lifting her head or opening her eyes.

John stood in place, hands on his hips and pursing his lips from left to right before continuing. "Hmm. I could have sworn I heard someone say something behind me. But when I turned around, no one was there."

"Did it have a German accent?" said Gretchen, mostly into the pillow.

"Not at all."

"Don't worry about it, then. Maybe it was the German guy's day off."

John came around the side of the bed to sit next to Gretchen. "I know you think I shouldn't pay much attention to my hearing things now and then, that I should brush it off because my neurologist says there is no residual damage from the accident. But if you heard what I heard, you wouldn't be so ready to dismiss it and go back to sleep—"

"Zzzzz."

"—which you obviously don't have any trouble doing."

John's most recent bout with hearing voices had come almost three years earlier when he was eating lunch by himself in the office break room, enjoying the latest issue of his favorite "Captain Whatever" comic book. In this issue, The Captain was battling a runty villain going by the less-than-terrorizing name of "The Gesticulator." The Gesticulator wanted revenge on the world for not being born tall, and for having hands that looked like angry ferrets after washing them in a barrel of nuclear waste that he'd mistaken for the bathroom sink. The Captain, whose strength was his all-powerful blasé attitude and to not give a damn about anything, was about to answer The Gesticulator's challenge with his famous "Yeah, whatever" knockout blow of disinterest, when John heard a disapproving voice from over his shoulder.

"Unt vhy are you read-ink shtoopid comic books vhen you could be read-ink sum-sing constructive like a software manual??" Predictably, John had spun around in his seat to find no one there, searching the room and then peering out from the kitchen door in search of a stranger. Left scratching his head, he kept the incident to himself until he got home that evening and excitedly told Gretchen of the event. She tried to be as understanding as she could, but chose not to dwell on it in light of John's continued testing as being in perfect health. The neurologist's instructions to the couple were to listen to and process the experience, but not to linger on it. It was the doctor's opinion that doing so would encourage the reoccurrence of such episodes.

"Mmmmm." Gretchen's purring in her near-sleep brought John back to the immediate present. In an instinctual motion, she stuck her right hand in the air, groping for any part of John she could gather in and bring closer to her. John took her hand, kissed the back of it, and gently put it back down at her side.

He rose to check the remainder of the apartment. The front door was still locked, but he opened it anyway to look for activity in the hallway. Finding nothing amiss in the hall, he gave a brief thought to inspecting under the doormat, but just as quickly stifled the notion. After unlocking and re-locking the door twice for certainty, he looked in again on Gretchen, who was now blissfully asleep.

"Hmm," he thought, "whatever it was, it was. It is early and I was excited and maybe Gretchen's right and blah blah blah—let's just get on with it, shall we?"

John slipped out of the bedroom and returned to his desk. Hoping to unwind from the knot he had tied himself into, he closed his eyes and let himself sink into his chair. He thought about going in and waking up

Gretchen again, this time on purpose so as to make passionate love to her. That was one thing that always put all of his life's consternation on hold. He imagined taking hold of her long, supple, freckle-covered body, enveloping her gangly frame in his own, and kissing her from head to toe with the sum of his affection. Then they would make love—a love so powerful, so overwhelming, that it would drown out any and all troubling voices, whether occurring in real life or of speculative origin.

Though the temptation to wake her was strong, John opted to let Gretchen catch up on the rest he had deprived her of when he went on his hunting expedition under the rug. In order to relax himself, he concentrated on nestling his being into her peaceable unconscious. He sang to her insides with everything he could think of that was right with their world, then sighed with satisfaction and smiled. After doing a fair job of calming himself, he almost fell asleep, finding a serene sanctuary in his affection. He had to forcibly pull himself out of his bliss by opening his eyes, taking a sip of his coffee, and then shaking out his cheeks with a resonant "RRRRRBBBBLNG" sound.

John rose and prepared himself for work. Thinking back to the Shuffling Mushroom announcement as he shaved, it did his soul good to know that the powers that be were not doing anything to possibly aid someone else in gaining even a toehold in his field of expertise. And it amounted to blessed relief to find out that there was nothing new he might have to learn.

He was good at what he did—his charts not only informed but somehow made one sense splendor in a most pure form because he or she had witnessed them. Learning something new, however, like being introduced to someone and having to remember their name, was for John his daily trek up Kilimanjaro in nothing but his bathroom slippers. However easy it was for him to break any ratio into a pie chart and transform it into a near-phantasmagoric display was balanced out by his difficulty in remembering names, places, directions, et al. He used his gifts to compensate for his shortcomings, ultimately figuring out workarounds to get him through the rough spots.

But all of his methodologies would prove to be of little to no use to him soon enough.

9

ASHEN ME
NO QUESTIONS

◐

SHRUGGING OFF THE EARLY morning's disconcerting events and focusing on the uplifting vocational news, John stepped out of his building and began on his crosstown walk to work. In what had become a game to him since the incident at Rug Nation, he took note of every trashcan he saw en route to his job. Waste bins had taken on a specific role in his life, a symbol of what was once wrong and now was right. For when John passed each trashcan, he made a mental note of its fullness, drawing a chart in his mind to measure the degree to which each bin was being used.

John even went so far as to assign a set of practical values to his ritual. For one, here was a largely unscientific but still notable glimpse into a pattern of waste usage and removal in the City. "Perhaps someone could use this study some day," he'd think to himself, all the while realizing the idea was as lame as a three-legged pony. He was not so lost in his mental meanderings as to think that anyone other than he would ever have any use for this information.

Second, counting the same bins each time provided him with a tracking system from his home to his work place. John lost his way in the streets easily, but tenaciously held presentation data like a baby with a lollipop in its sticky-fingered grip.

Finally, even after some ten years had passed, John thrilled to be able to keep track of not one but sixteen trashcans which dotted the landscape of his route. Sometimes he almost wished he would run into Peg McElroy on this walk and proudly profile for her the status of every trashcan within a ten block radius. Peg had lodged in John's mind as a watershed with short-cropped hair and a plastic smile, enabling John to keep her memory alive along with the recollection of her name. But usually about the time that he remembered her name he would wonder if she would recall him, or even get the connection. "Yeah, she'd probably just be weirded out," he thought. It was usually at that point that he quit wishing he would run into Peg McElroy.

John arrived at his workplace twenty minutes late. An old tan stone warehouse building, the structure had recently been renovated to feature a cavernous lobby, shiny new banks of elevators, and the latest technical accoutrements in hopes of luring the city's sexiest successful businesses to relocate there. Although he was well aware management didn't care when he came or left just as long as he got the job done—which he always did— he still couldn't escape a nagging, irrational fear of rebuke. And on this particular morning the feeling became unusually oppressive the closer he got to his office building. Once he figured in the final trashcan, wrapped up the morning's data collection, and caught sight of the front door of his workplace on lower Fifth Avenue, the sensation became visceral. He was used to feeling harried and a touch nervous until he got to his desk. But this was a dizzying, nauseous sensation unlike anything he'd ever known.

He finally paused ten feet in front of the lobby doors, leaned over to put his hands on his knees, and shook his head vigorously.

"What the heck did I eat for breakfast? Did I drink too much last night? Did I forget I was sick and that I haven't gotten over it yet? Jeezus, what the... "

These questions thrashed and banged around inside John like a pandemonium of parrots suddenly aware that they'd been stolen from the Amazon and were now locked up in some private aviary. He dropped to his knees and took a couple of deep breaths of the chill morning air, returning the air to the environment in brief, vaporous sighs. It was then that a gruff but compassionate male voice spoke to him from above his station.

"Hey pal, I know you don't feel so good right now, but you'll be all right before you can say 'Jack Robinson.' Like anyone's gonna say that out of the blue: 'Hey whaddaya want for lunch?' 'I dunno—Jack Robinson?' I don't think so. Anyway, just give me another hour or so and I'll be right with you."

"I'm all right. I must've eaten something or maybe I've been sick, I don't know—hey!"

It had taken a moment for John to recognize the voice he imagined hearing earlier that morning. He stood up in a shot to see who had addressed him, jerking his head in every direction. But there was no one in sight. He screwed up his face, squinting as he scanned the area.

"Crazy. Just plain crazy. Maybe I have been ill."

What he also thought crazy was that all of a sudden he felt a bit better. So he decided that he might as well head inside. He gave one last fleeting thought as to who had spoken to him, and then cleared his throat and flexed his shoulders so as to signal his current fitness to anyone nearby who might be evaluating his condition.

John made his way through the glass doors and negotiated the crowded lobby. He glided past some while bounced off other workers scurrying to get to their respective destinations. He less than gently bounced off one such scurrier.

"Hey slow down buddy—you almost made me drop my coffee," said a portly middle-aged man in a dark blue tie, white button down shirt, and khaki slacks, carrying a tray of two coffees and several donuts decorated far too early for the holidays with red, green, and white sprinkles. John stopped for a brief moment to look the man up and down with a gaze that at least partially contained a feeling of awe.

"Did you say that? Did you say that to me?" John asked, his eyes wide with recognition.

"Sure I did. You wanna make something of it? I'll toss this tray in your face—"

John took a step toward the man and grasped his arms.

"No, no, don't do that. I'm really very sorry to have almost knocked the tray out of your hand. But you don't know what it means to me that you're actually standing there. Can I give you some money?"

The man with the tray not so gently shook off John's hands and slowly began to back away from John.

"That's all right," said the donut man, continuing to back up cautiously, "you just stay where you are. And watch where you're going." The man turned around as quickly as he could without risk of dropping the tray unassailed and fled with this meal, disappearing in the morning crowd.

Still not feeling anything like one hundred percent, but relieved to have had a living, breathing stranger address him in a readily identifiable fashion, John squeezed into the elevator up to his floor. He whisked through the lobby at Hadfield, giving a cursory "Good morning" to the receptionist. Upon arriving at his cubicle, his co-worker, Todd Johnson, stood up and popped his head out of his neighboring stall.

"Good morning, your chartness," said Todd, bowing slightly and rolling his right hand down from his chin to his navel in a mock address to royalty. Johnson had honed his techno-geek jadedness to near-perfection, delivering each sentence as flatly as humanly possible. He was wearing one of his favorite t-shirts which read in large letters "I AM IT" and then directly below in much smaller print, "AND YOU ARE NOT." Most people did not get that "IT" referred to his job as an Information Technology specialist. Consequently, most thought Todd self-centered to an offensive and unhealthy degree. This perception suited Todd just fine.

And though technically he was listed as an IT specialist, Todd's real job was to look after everything John. Todd made sure John's computer and printer were working, that he had enough yellow pads, that he had enough pens and pencils and that those pencils were sharpened—that John's world was running like a finely-oiled machine. Through the years, Todd had built or customized many of the programs John used to produce his work. Yet what John ultimately produced with Todd's programming dumbfounded and mystified the IT professional. What the programmer had coded or customized wasn't supposed to do what John made it do.

For instance, Todd's code was supposed to produce a simple blue sphere on screen, nothing more. Yet for one pitch his agency was making for an eco-tourism company, John took those same computer instructions and created a blue, Earth-like planet with continents pulsing to the beat of a disco version of "By The Beautiful Sea." And if that wasn't enough, the planet was orbited by several multi-colored moons with smiling faces, heartily enjoying the continents' rhythmic undulations.

That particular graphic trick had astounded Todd so that he checked the underlying compiled output code of that presentation. What Todd saw made no sense whatsoever in terms of conventional programming. It was so convoluted that whatever John had plugged in should've crashed the machine, at best, and really should have fried the whole operating system. Todd found this so bewildering that it was the last time he ever ventured to look into John's output code.

Todd watched John put his coat on the back of his chair and settle in for the work day. After a moment, Todd tried to engage John once more, still standing by his cubicle wall.

"So what's cooking, charts n' crafts?"

"Same old, same old, friend."

"It's Todd."

"Yeah, I know, or know forty seven percent of the time but which percentage drops precipitously if you're only considering morning exchanges. What can I say?"

"Not my name, but I'd never hold that against you. Anyway, it's not your brain concerning me at the moment. You having a rough morning?"

"No. Why?"

"Because you look like shit."

"But I feel fine."

"Don't lie. I know you. I can see it in your face."

"I'm okay," responded John, starting to feel unnerved again.

"Uh-uh. You look like shit. In fact, your face is a public service announcement to stay out of shit town."

"I'm fine."

"No. You look like the latest victim of a shit-sylvanian vampire attack.

"Stop—"

"In the royal gardens of shit, your face is coming up roses."

"That doesn't even make any sense."

"Okay look, all I'm saying is that you don't seem like your normal self, or abnormal self—whichever you prefer."

"Well all right," John said, "I guess I am feeling a little funky. Some weird stuff's been happening this morning and I can't really explain it, Tom. No I mean Ted-Tim-TAD—"

"Todd. The last one was close."

John shook his head in disgust. "Christ, it's not like I don't want to remember your name. You'd think since I've known you almost as long as Gretchen…"

"Gretchen is your girlfriend. No offense, but I'm glad you don't think of me in that way. What you should think about is turning around and going home. You look… I don't know how to put it exactly. How about… ashen? Yeah, that sounds about right. You look ashen."

Todd leaned into his cubicle, grabbed his iced coffee, and spoke again only after he had taken a sizeable gulp and sounded a clarion of a burp intended to disgust anyone within earshot.

"Okay then. I got some work to finish up before the big presentation at ten. Drop today's chartismo supremos on the server, and then get the fuck outta here."

With that, Todd disappeared behind the divider between the two cubicles.

"'Ashen?' Hmm." John nervously tried to settle himself into his workspace, but was unsuccessful in shaking off his co-worker's last descriptor. Something about the word unnerved him, like an itch on his back just out of reach of scratching range of either hand.

"Who the hell looks 'ashen?'" he silently asked the gray screen before him, which was currently monitoring his computer's startup process. Unsurprisingly getting no response, he repeated the phrase again, but this time out loud. Todd shot up in his cubicle.

"You need something, Leon Chartsky?" said Todd over the cubicle wall.

Not realizing that he had made his last thought audible and surprised at hearing Todd's voice, John popped out of his seat like a brand new Jack-in-the-box.

"Woah—now that's what I call an up-start." remarked Todd, looking up from his chair.

"What? Oh, yeah. I guess I am feeling a bit edgy."

"Homeward bound, then?" asked Todd.

"Nah, not just yet, maybe later. It's not every day you get to feel ashen, now, is it? Heh."

"Yup. You're what you'd call a real ash-tronaut."

"What?"

"Forget it."

"Oh, right. Funny, sort of. Hey, I'm going to the men's room. Gonna throw some water on my face and see if I can liven myself up some."

"Sure, man. Wash that shit off your puss. Gray isn't your color."

John could see the men's room sign over the tops of the cubicles, and so he had no problem finding it on a regular basis. As he crossed the office, he mulled the word over in his mind over and over, moving it around inside of him but finding no suitable place to put it down safely. Ashen.

Having successfully navigated his passage to the lavatory, John opened the heavy door and cautiously approached the large mirror which spanned the width of the two bathroom sinks. He nervously peered from outside the near edge of the mirror, slowly bringing his entire upper body into view. Once he was satisfied that there were going to be no further surprises in his reflection, he leaned in to observe himself closely in the mirror. He lightly scratched his chin, and screwed up his face as if making sure all the parts were in order.

"'Ashen', huh," John said to his reflected twin. He noticed an almost lurid pastiness to his complexion that no other single word he could think of did justice. "You know, I *do* look ashen."

Just then the sound of a toilet flushing behind John interrupted his self-examination. Once again, John did his dance of faux relaxation, only this time he was at least partially justified in feeling ill at ease with himself.

From the left stall emerged Jaagup Kukk, a heavyset Estonian émigré who worked in accounting, hardly done with zipping up his fly and fastening his belt as he pushed open the stall door. Jaagup swung from side to side as he exited the stall, regaining his balance as he took his first steps out into the main area. He pressed under his right armpit an open copy of *International Accountant,* his favorite magazine next to the

Estonian edition of *Maxim*. Jaagup had hoped to finish reading an adventure story about an accountant in Romania who, using a nuclear-powered TI-77X 6-line scientific calculator with missile intercept and safe-cracking capabilities, had single-handedly broken up a diabolical spy ring.

"Ah, Johnny, talking to yourself?" Jaagup said, balancing the magazine while tucking in his shirt, his belt still undone. "No reason to feel shame. I talk to self all the time. And you know, most times I really like what I say. I make a lot of sense to me, you know?"

"But I don't generally talk to myself—"

Jaguup raised his palm out in front of him, waving off John's remonstration. "Please. No apologize. You're good boy, Johnny."

"I know, it's just that I'm not feeling one hundred percent."

"One hundred percent? Who feels one hundred percent? Crazy people. They the only ones."

"I suppose so."

"But say—" Jaagup had finally managed to tuck in most of his shirt and redo his belt without dropping the magazine to the floor. "—you really don' look so good. Maybe you go home."

"That seems to be the popular sentiment."

"Or go for walk. Get out of here. This room for deep thought only."

With that, Jaagup stepped back from John, looked in the mirror, and ran through a quick mental checklist of things to do before leaving the bathroom. He stopped at item number three, discovering that he had forgotten to zip up his fly. He pulled up the zipper slowly, making sure he did not injure himself in the process as he had done recently, resulting in an awkward and painful visit to the hospital ER.

His manly apparatus safely secured, Jaagup took his leave of the washroom. John assumed Jaagup's place in front of the mirror.

"Okay. Enough of this. The man's right. I need some fresh air."

Back at his desk, John was quick to put on his coat. Todd peered over the top of his cubicle.

"Where're you goin', Char-tagnan?"

"For a walk."

"A good idea. But not just yet."

"Why not?" replied John, barely concealing his increasing irritation.

"The charts, kind sir, the charts. The meeting's in a half an hour and you uncharacteristically have yet to deliver me the goods."

"Oh yeah, right. The charts. Here."

John hit a key that launched a system macro sending his latest work over to Todd's computer. Todd's machine bonged in receipt of the file.

The graphics John had prepared for the presentation opened on Todd's computer monitor in a four tile arrangement, yet to Todd and others who quickly came to gather around the computer screen, the charts appeared almost holographic and spinning in space.

Todd's jaw dropped in awe. "Jesus Christ, will you look at those charts!" The only time Todd would lose his über-geek coolness was when he got a first look at John's work. Being a senior programmer, Todd considered it a duty to appear unimpressed by anything technical he had not created himself, but when it came to John's work he lost all self-control.

His face now inches from the screen, Todd sat transfixed by the perceived holographic nature of the four charts. When he hovered his cursor over a chart slice, that slice appeared to lift out of the whole and exhibit some quality of the elements of earth, air, fire, and water. What was more, Todd could swear that he actually felt changes to his environment as he highlighted various components of the chart.

"Hey John, not only are your charts smokin' as always, this time they're actually smokin'! Does anyone else smell it? These things are on fire. Holy what-the-fuck, man. Every time I think you've done it all, you go and one-up yourself. One-up? Christ, you've ten-upped yourself, a hundred-upped—" Todd's mind raced with attempted connections to the software and what the software produced. But, as always, he would find himself lacking for words.

"Seriously, dude, this is gonna knock 'em dead."

Todd turned from the screen.

"John?"

But John was already gone, in the elevator, heading straight down.

10

A MONUMENTAL
STROLL

◑

J OHN STOOD IN THE elevator with his overcoat collar turned up, doing what he could to ignore his fellow passengers' sidelong glances. But before the doors could open to the first floor, John lost whatever vestige he had left of his composure and fitfully clawed his way to the front of the car. The dust of morbid curiosity that had settled over the car quickly turned to anger.

"What's the hurry?" asked a tall salesman with combed-over thinning hair in a tweed coat. John had almost caused the man's overstuffed, worn brown sales briefcase to become unlatched in his push to the front of the elevator.

"Just wait 'til one day when you look ashen!" hollered John, not turning around as he made for the front door.

"What the hell is he talking about? Did anyone understand what he was talking about?" asked the man in the tweed coat of his fellow passengers exiting the elevator, before he, like the other riders, moved on and let the incident dissipate without further notice in the scrambling current of the workday morning.

Once outside, John moved quickly to avoid any more unwanted scrutiny. He arbitrarily turned to walk uptown on Fifth Avenue, as the difference between uptown and downtown was lost on him, especially in his agitated state.

Wishing to do whatever he could to shield his face, he stopped to buy a baseball cap from a street vendor. He quickly chose a black cap with the lettering BROOKLYN stitched in white on the front. Anything Brooklyn-related was an easy sell with John, as he had never forgotten the night of his subway ride there and the profound effect it had on his life.

He proffered a new twenty-dollar bill to the street vendor, a middle-aged Asian man of medium height and build whose face bore the grooves of many a day braving harsh winter winds to hawk his wares. The vendor was preoccupied with quickly taking hats off the sales table and replacing them with others, as if he could gauge the personality of the passing throng and what hats they would most likely buy. He paused momentarily to push his palm straight out at John and his money.

"No charge for you. Your hat paid for already."

"Excuse me?"

"Man come by here five minutes ago. He say funny-looking man will buy BROOKLYN hat. So he pay for it up front. You funny-looking enough. You look like rubber chicken with bad paint job. And you buy Brooklyn hat. So have nice day. Next customer, please."

"Funny-looking?"

"Yeah. He pretty funny-looking too, though not like you. He your father?"

"My father lives in Ohio. There's been some sort of mistake."

"Well then you win free hat. Next customer."

An elderly woman with a floral patterned scarf tied around her head, who had been patiently waiting to this point for John's business to be completed, edged her way in front of John to speak to the vendor.

"Excuse me, young man." Her voice was more irritated than polite.

"But—"

By now the vendor and the woman had begun haggling about the price of a scarf. John numbly put the cap on his head and turned away. He tried to make sense of the incident with the hat vendor, which pre-empted his will to keep moving and left him standing still in the middle of the sidewalk. He remained there some moments until a construction worker in a hardhat—the size of a small building himself—bumped into him, transferring gray construction dust onto John's coat in the process.

"Hey pal, what's your problem?" said the construction worker gruffly. "Maybe you missed it but they nixed the proposal to make this a private sidewalk."

"Okay, sorry. I was just—"

But the construction worker had already moved on. John yanked down the brim of the cap, dusted himself off as best he could, and headed down the street.

He walked a dozen or more blocks, hoping the sun's rays and his body's movement would foster some improvement. But he felt worse, if anything. So he ducked his head into the first pay phone he came across, and pulled a small handful of change from his left pants pocket. He also took a small address book from his coat, and thumbed through it nervously until he got to the "G" page and he found the number for "GRETCHEN (WORK)." He put a quarter in the slot and nervously hit the numbers on the metal key pad. The phone rang twice before there was an answer.

"Gretchen Sweeney's office. Melissa speaking. How can I help you?" Melissa Sundberg was Gretchen's personable Executive Assistant.

"Yes you can. Gretchen Sweeney, please."

"Is this John? Hi John!"

"Hello—" Melissa cut off John before he could flounder with remembering Melissa's name. They had met at Gretchen's office holiday party the previous year, and John had been very personable in discussing his work while deftly avoiding land mines like names, places, and the like. "You know I was just thinking about you," continued Melissa, "the guy who does our PowerPoint stuff's work really sucks. I could do better, and I just learned the program two months ago. Some people like the guy's graphics and the work's functional and all, but to me it blows the Big Kahuna. It's chartjunk, mostly. Gretchen's shown me your stuff, and it's frigging a-mazing—"

"Thank you very much," said John, who had been thinking of how little he thought of the PowerPoint program, and how people used it as a weak substitute for genuine analytical interpretation and presentation. "Um, can I just please speak to Gretchen?"

"Why sure." Not altogether privy to John's ways, Melissa was put off by his abrupt query, taking his ill-at-ease for unexpected rudeness. "One moment, please." Melissa put the call through to Gretchen in her office.

"Good morning, Threatening Carpet Corporation. How can I help you?"

"Yeah, hi. It's me."

"Yes, I know," said Gretchen, disappointed John was not up for a few moments' playful banter. "Melissa told me."

"Who's Melissa?"

"She's my assistant. You've met her a few times."

"She seemed upset."

"She's upset because you've talked with her at length and she thinks you're cool. I've shown her some of your work." Gretchen paused. "People don't understand why you don't remember them. But don't worry about it; I'll explain it to her. How are you, sweetie?"

"Not so good, actually."

"What do you mean? And where are you calling me from, anyway? I hear street noise."

"I'm out on Fifth Avenue."

Gretchen was now alarmed. "Out on Fifth Avenue? Why are you out on Fifth Avenue?"

"I'm taking a walk. I don't feel well. I went out to get some air. The popular consensus is that I look ashen."

"Out taking a walk? 'Ashen?' What does that even mean?"

"I look sort of pasty and everything about me just looks off. I feel off. I wouldn't be surprised if something fell off."

"You mean you're that sick and you're out taking a walk? Why didn't you take a cab home?" said Gretchen.

"I didn't think it was serious. It feels more serious now."

"Oh god. And you're on Fifth Avenue? What's the cross street?"

"I think it says..." John took a couple of steps out onto the sidewalk and squinted to read the street sign on the corner. "...28th Street. Yeah—28th Street. I've been this way once or twice before, even though I know I usually head straight across to our place. I mean, I'm pretty sure I've been this way—"

"You're 'pretty sure?' That's because you've been that way with me when I came to pick you up after work. Oh Jeezus. Please, sweetheart, just stay where you are."

"I can do that."

"That's good. I mean it's not good that you're feeling sick but it's good that you're not going to move. The last time you went to get a little air I ended up finally tracking you down at Grant's Tomb."

Gretchen's comment caused John to reach back into his mind and download a file containing the fuzzy but pleasant memory of his excursion to Grant's Tomb. He remembered that it wasn't a complete accident that he had ended up there, as he had been interested in visiting that President's final resting place for some time. He took refuge in the browser of his consciousness and surfed the web of his mind to where years before he had been contracted to work up a chart correlating the New York City's most-visited monuments and the cost of construction for each. The study itself revealed little to no useful information, but of course the charts were a hit. John had recognized that this was among his best work. The evening of the presentation he was looking for something to do while he waited for Gretchen to arrive home from work late. He recalled projecting the charts onto the living room wall of his apartment.

Seated in the darkness and drinking a glass of red wine, he had watched chart slices indicating the various monuments spin and dance in the air. He had then selected the slice representing Grant's tomb, which prompted a hologram of a saber fight between a Union blue and a Confederacy gray uniform, complete with sword clanging sound effects. In each uniform fought a translucent, ghost-like soldier, each of whom John had wished he had been able to imbue with more expressiveness as he battled. But beyond his regrets in regard to the limited emotional palette, John sat back and soaked in the two phantoms battling in the cold projected light.

That night John felt a deep satisfaction watching the duel, and he held his glass aloft in salute to the two phantasmagorical fighting men. Life had been good, at least for that moment.

Life wasn't so good right now.

"John? John, are you still there?" Gretchen's distressed voice closed the browser window in his mind.

"I'm here."

You just wait right where you are, sweetheart. I'm coming to get you."

"I'm not going anywhere," he replied.

11

COME PLAY
IN TRAFFIC

◑

WAITING FOR GRETCHEN TO arrive, John wedged himself into the niche in the facade of a nearby building as best he could. In darting movements, he tried to be inconspicuous while at the same time exposing his face in an effort to give it some color. The sum total of his actions gave him the appearance of a flasher, except the only thing he was flashing was his ashen face.

John tried to think of something pleasant and altogether foreign to his current predicament. He thought of the night on the subway, and thought of Gretchen. He even did his best to conjure how good he felt the night he watched his monuments presentation in his apartment. He searched his mind for anything that might afford him a feeling of relief. Finally, he ceased his peek-a-boo-with-the-public routine, leaned back up against the wall, stared out on to the Avenue, and surrendered himself to the flow. This strategy was actually starting to work, as he was taken by an almost surprising calm.

It was then that John eyed some unusual movement on his vision's periphery. He tipped up the brim of his cap a touch and turned his head to the right to see what might be causing the stir.

There, in the middle of Fifth Avenue, seemingly oblivious to the traffic around him, stood a man of five and a half feet in a well-worn brown corduroy sport jacket and brown pants that almost matched. To say he was pudgy would be more than fair; he looked as if one could rearrange his cushiony features any which way without too much trouble. The man's jacket was styled with disproportionately peaked lapels, the tips of which were so tall that their fabric toppled earthward, unable to support their ridiculous size and weight. He wore a pork pie hat in yet another shade of brown, and was actively engaged in looking out for someone or something far down the Avenue.

John was about to file this in his unconscious journal of things mildly amusing and then quickly forgotten when the man was run over by a red Lamborghini going full speed.

John's initial sense of shock gave way to awe, as the man sprung back up as if he had been a wooden duck shot down at a carnival game booth and reset by the operator. Once upright, the man dusted himself off with his hat, replaced it on his head, and then turned to yell after the Lamborghini driver, who was now far down the avenue and out of sight. He cupped his hands over his mouth, as if this would make it easier for the long gone driver to hear him.

"Why don't you watch where you're goin', asshole? Just because you got a fancy Italian shmallion car doesn't mean you own the road. Schmuck..."

Appraising his condition further, the man took off his hat to brush the remaining dust from his clothing, all the while continuing his Sisyphean task of trying to get his lapels to stay upright. Once he had dusted himself off to his general satisfaction, and had made three or four fruitless passes at the lapels, he returned to his vigil of looking up the avenue, disgusted yet resigned.

"I tell you, some people... " He waved at nothing in particular, all the while dodging ensuing vehicles by bending his legs like giant rubber bands from one side to the other, sidestepping any further head-on collisions.

Along with observing the indecipherable strangeness of the proceedings, John also became aware that he was the only person who seemed to notice what was going on. And even though the man was out in the middle of the street, separated from John by the entirety of the foot traffic on the sidewalk, he could hear everything the man said, right down to the man's last grumbled "Schmuck" pronouncement.

At the same moment that John recognized the peculiar clarity of the sound, the man turned in John's direction, and began motioning for John to come stand with him at his tenuous location in the middle of Fifth Avenue.

John scanned about himself to see if perhaps the man was beckoning someone else in his immediate vicinity. But no, it appeared that the man was directing his attention at John, and when he pointed his left index finger at his chest, the man on the Avenue nodded emphatically, waving again for John to come join him.

The man with the prodigiously peaked lapels continued to bend his body left and right with an absurd elasticity, like he was executing an exaggerated hula hoop routine, minus the hula hoop. His face, however, bore no sign that he was playing a game, as he switched his attention back and forth between looking up the Avenue and then at John, becoming increasingly impatient with the latter.

The man then stretched his arm out in John's direction, lifting it over traffic so as to avoid sticking it through someone's car window. He snaked his limb over the heads of passersby on the sidewalk, and brought it to a stop right in front of John's face. With his palm facing up he curled his forefinger, beckoning John to come out onto the Avenue.

His eyes popping like two misshapen marbles, John, focusing on the extended digit, feverishly shook his head "No."

Unhappy with John's response, the man in the outsized lapels reeled in the inviting arm, put both hands on his hips, and made a zigzag dash for John, bending himself around and above the traffic en route.

Arriving at John's spot on the sidewalk, the man shoved his face right up to John's as if he was a baseball manager arguing a bad call with an umpire. The man further fulfilled this description when he tweaked John's hat, pushing it a few inches to the left as he laid into John.

"What the heck do you think you're doing? Do you think I'm standing out there because I like it?" The man paused in his rant to look away for a moment. "Come to think of it, I *do* like it, but that's beside the point." He then turned his attention back to John. Why didn't you meet me out there when I called for you?"

"I-I didn't want to get killed," responded John, almost numb with fear.

The man sighed, pushing up his lapels. Immediately upon their release, the lapels drooped right back down. "What, did you see me getting 'killed' out there? You just go with the flow."

John didn't reply, thinking that avoiding onrushing traffic by twisting his body about wasn't a flow in which he could go.

"Well, anyway, we gotta get goin'. You can trust me or my name isn't Sam Sloan—a nice economical, two-syllable job. It's like Sam Spade. You know, the private dick in that flick *The Maltese Falcon*. Except when you drop the 'S' in his name you get 'PADE', and with me you're only gettin' a 'LOAN.' Get it?"

John looked at Sam Sloan just as blankly as ever.

"Nah, I didn't think so. No one ever gets it, not unless I write it down for them. What're you gonna do? That's show business."

Sam turned to walk back out into the street. When John didn't follow, Sam remarked "Whah, no one ever told you to go play in traffic? C'mon."

Sam stepped off of the sidewalk, and would've been mowed down by a speeding Toyota if his legs hadn't bowed upward and outward into the shape of the vehicle, allowing it to pass. He returned to his station in the middle of the road.

"C'mon—I'm gettin' lonely out here."

Again, Sam's voice could be heard clearly through the automobile and human traffic, and John was quick to answer it. "I'm not going out th—"

Before John could finish his sentence, Sam shot out his arm some thirty-five feet again, wrapping his arm around John's waist, and reeling him into the road like a giant lizard's tongue snapping up a fly. Sam held John out four feet from his side and two feet off the ground.

On the precipice of going into shock, John shivered in abject fear. "How...w-w-why are you doing this to me?"

Sam peered down the Avenue for whatever it was that he was looking for. He addressed John while maintaining his lookout.

"Just try to relax, which I know is easy for me to say. Of course right now things look pretty cockamamie. But don't worry about anyone else seeing you. Nobody can see you as long as you're tied up here, so to speak. And if I can just get some help, we should be done before you can say—well, just say whatever you want to say. Anyway, the truck should be here any minute."

"Truck?" echoed John.

"Yeah. Nice couple of guys driving it. You'll love 'em. Sure, and Liberace worked on the side as a pro wrestler."

Enjoying his own sarcasm, Sam let out a short, loud "Hah!" while simultaneously hoisting John above a passing Range Rover. Maintaining his lookout for the truck, he dipped and dangled John in and out of the way of all passing vehicles, bringing John from within an inch of the street and then up in the air in all directions.

"I'm gonna puke." John could hardly get the words out.

"You're gonna have to speak up, kid. My hearing ain't what it used to be. Plus there's a lotta traffic today. I think the President's in town, or maybe Trump is getting new hair delivered, or some other bullshit. Who knows? Nobody tells me anything."

"I—I—"

With those two pronouns, John ceased communication through regular speech, and let his stomach do the talking. He emptied his insides in explosive fashion, spraying the street, Sam's arm, and the windshield of a powder blue Chevy, suddenly and thoroughly mystifying the driver.

This display managed to get Sam's attention.

"Aww, for the love of Shirley! And I just had this jacket pressed. I guess I didn't make it clear that if some part of you loses contact with me—like your breakfast there—it becomes visible. Well, too late now."

Instantly a tiny white, front loading, washing machine appeared around Sam's sullied sleeve area, his arm going horizontally through the center of the unit. A gentle wash cycle was immediately initiated, while Sam continued maneuvering John in and out of the way of passing cars and maintaining his lookout for the truck, which he was relieved to see finally coming down the street. He clapped his hands together enthusiastically, which involved swinging John and the washing machine back and forth some twenty feet.

"Okay! Now we're in business! I didn't want to tell you, but these guys are usually a lot later than the ten minutes they already are. The boys have picked up the pace."

John could not share in Sam's elation, as he was now unconscious, pushed over the edge by being swung about in Sam's exultant handclap. Upon recognizing this, Sam's enthusiasm turned to disappointment.

"Nuts! And I promised myself this one was going to go smooth. I could kick myself. Oh right, I can."

Sam stretched his left leg out some ten feet, cranked it up like an old wind-up toy, and uncoiled it in a flash to deliver himself a swift kick to his own rear.

It was then that the large commercial delivery truck, with the single word **SUPPLIES** emblazoned on its sides in black block letters, approached where Sam was standing. Although in some bygone day the truck must have been white, the truck was now a dingy, dirty gray. It ran a red light—along with passing through several vehicles—and came to a screeching halt next to Sam in the middle of the Avenue.

With the sound of the truck's brakes being applied, all activity within sight came to an abrupt and total stop, except for Sam and the now limp John. At the same time, the washing machine disappeared from Sam's sleeve, and a new brown Naugahyde La-Z-Boy recliner chair materialized in the road.

Employing a hitherto unseen gentleness, Sam set John down in the chair, as if putting a sleeping baby down in its crib, then snapped back his arm to normal length. He paused a moment to regard John in the recliner with what only could be interpreted as genuine concern. Sam sighed once, and then re-extended his arm to grab and push the wooden lever on the side of the chair all the way down so as to set it in its fully reclining state. Once John's body appeared settled and he began to snore, Sam reeled back in his arm again and stuck both hands on his hips, further taking in the scene. He then spoke to John with affection, not that John or anyone in the immediate vicinity was in a position to appreciate his tenderness.

"Okay, kid. I know that was a rough ride. But I'm gonna make it up to you. I can promise you that." John curled more tightly into a fetal ball, and his lips fluttered in a particularly emphatic snore. Miraculously, John's hat still sat on his head, albeit slightly cockeyed after his swinging ordeal.

"Yeah, you said it." Sam then straightened the hat on John's head, and turned in the direction of the truck. He took a half a step before snapping the fingers of his right hand in front of him.

"Oh yeah—right," he said, executing a quick one-eighty to place his hand on John's head once more, spreading out his fingers over the top of his skull. "That should take the bite outta this."

Grunting and shifting slightly in the chair, it almost appeared that John responded to Sam's touch and words of assurance. But if he did, it was somewhere deep within, as he remained unconscious.

Satisfied with John's condition, Sam returned to preparing himself for his rendezvous with the newly arrived vehicle. After pulling down his shirt collar, tightening up his weathered blue and brown diagonal stripe patterned necktie, throwing back his shoulders, cocking his hat forward, and making one more futile attempt at getting his lapels to stay upright, he headed for the truck's cab. "Now comes fun time."

12

PRICKS OF INDIFFERENCE

◑

S AM CROSSED BEHIND THE truck to get to the driver's side, and then strode up to the cab with at least a veneer of resolute confidence. The tinted windows blocked any view into the driver's compartment. He stood beside the cab for a moment, rocking on his heels, holding his lapels with his thumbs pointing upward, waiting for someone to stir in the truck. Thinking to himself: "Like I got nothin' better to do than stand here and whistle 'Dixie,'" he began to loudly whistle the tune in the direction of the driver's window. Eliciting no response, he cleared his throat at an exaggerated volume, and then again twice more at five second intervals.

Finally, having exhausted his reserve of politeness, Sam yelled up at the cab: "Okay you clowns, quit making out in there! Open up and let's get cranking."

The tinted window rolled down, and the driver—a man looking like a young Santa Claus in Santa's lesser-known Hells Angels days, with a great wiry black beard carpeting most of his face and Ray-Ban sunglasses covering the rest of it—stuck his head out. He wore a black baseball cap with the slogan "BORN TO DIE" printed on the front in block lettering filled with a bright orange and red flame pattern. The driver's cheeks bulged with a full third of a liverwurst sandwich, a meal with which he seemed in no rush to finish.

"Hey Sam—you know what kind of a prick you are?" said the driver, not turning in Sam's direction, pushing his words out and around his chewing.

"No, Harry, I don't know what kind of a prick I am. Oh wait. I must be a 'prick-up truck' because I am generally not a prick except when I have to deal with you." Sam paused to appreciate his own joke. "Hey, that wasn't bad if slightly corny. All I need is a rimshot." On cue, a rimshot sounded from an indeterminate spot somewhere above them. "Thank you, thank you very much. I can't say I'll be here all week, but with these guys on the job, you never know."

Harry nodded his head, smiled slightly, and swallowed the portion of his sandwich he had been working on. "That's pretty funny. You're a regular comedian." He turned his head to the right to address an unseen figure in the cabin's passenger's seat. "Ain't that right, Stu? I mean, pricks don't make you laugh in general—that's why they're pricks. But Sam's a sometimes-funny prick, don't you think?"

"That's right. He's a sometimes-funny prick," answered Stu phlegmatically.

Harry turned his head back, and this time he shifted his gaze out the window to speak to Sam. "Y'see? Even Stu knows you're a sometimes-funny prick. Funny you don't know it."

"Remind me to take a self-awareness course sometime," answered Sam. "Now if you're finished with whatever you're stuffing your face with, perhaps you and your palsy-walsy can get around to doing your job. Then we can kiss and say goodbye."

Harry said something to his partner barely audible outside of the cab, and Sam heard the passenger door opening, followed by the sound of feet making contact with the ground. The door slammed shut, and unhurried footsteps moving in the direction of the rear of the truck echoed in the silence.

"The Stu-ster'll start the unload. I'll be back there in a sec' to finish up and to do the paperwork." Harry then pushed the final third of his sandwich into his mouth.

"Don't rush yourself," said Sam, "I wouldn't want you to choke."

Harry smiled and nodded, looking straight out ahead of him.

Sam headed for the back, where he found Stu perched on the edge of the truck body, ready to open the liftgate. Although thin, Stu was all sinewy muscle and looked like someone who could swiftly knife you in the gut and conceal the blade again before you could scream the "N" in "NOOO!" His hair was slicked back in place like it hadn't been disturbed in decades, and he showed a salt and pepper two-day stubble of beard. He wore his delivery uniform loosely; black jeans and a black T-shirt which bore the same white "SUPPLIES" logo as on the side of the truck. A freshly lit cigarette hung from the side of his mouth as if glued there. He wore no hat, but kept a fresh cigarette at the ready over his left ear.

"Those things can kill you, you know," said Sam, pointing at the cigarette.

Stu offered a faint but appreciative smile, and grabbed the rear liftgate handle to raise the metal gate with him. "You never stop, do you, Sam?"

After the initial heave, the paneled liftgate rattled open largely of its own accord to reveal the contents of the truck.

There in the large compartment stood all of one paneled exterior wooden door, painted white, framed like it was set up as a display item in a home improvement store showroom. Helium-filled balloons were tied to its frame with multi-colored ribbons, imprinted with **SALE!,** **HAPPY 4TH OF JULY!,** or variants on the American flag Stars-and-Stripes theme.

Dumbstruck, Sam looked at the door, and then peered in and around the sides of it. Not seeing anything else, he again made his right arm elastic and probed around the interior of the eighteen-foot storage compartment. He snapped back his arm and turned to Stu with a look of incredulity.

"Is this some kind of joke?" he said.

A loud belch answered Sam's question, followed by Harry's appearance from the left side of the truck.

"We don't do jokes, Sammy. That's your department." Harry held a clipboard with a few papers in his right hand. With his left, he wiped the last of his sandwich's breadcrumbs from his sizeable paunch.

"Don't tell me you got a problem," cautioned Stu. Stu's cigarette bobbed up and down as if it was a cantilevered, organic component of his oral framework. His whole demeanor was such that if Sam answered in the positive, the deliveryman could be given to sudden and brutal violence.

"A problem?" said Sam. "Why should there be a problem? I just need a standard issue inter-dimensional portal, and you show up with some sort of discount handyman's special. No problem at all."

Harry folded his arms. "They're backed up on regular portals at the plant. We got a couple of refurbs due at the end of the week, but what you're looking at is the best we can do today."

Sam took a step back and rubbed his chin. "'Refurbs,' huh? 'End of the week,' huh? And I'm supposed to use that," he said, pointing at the item on the truck.

Standing next to the door, Stu took a quick look at the unit and kicked it a couple of times, an impromptu demonstration of its solid construction.

"What, are you guys nuts? I gotta kid over there—" Sam pointed to John, still very much unconscious in the La-Z-Boy "—whom I've been commissioned to bring in Special Delivery, and you expect me to use that desecration of a perfectly good tree?"

Stu peered out from the corner of the open truck and looked back at Sam.

"Nice chair, Sammy. Where'd you get it, if I might ask?"

"I brought it from the office."

"Lemme see this chair." Harry brushed right by Sam and went over to John and the piece of furniture in question. He ran his hand over the surface of the living room accessory, judging it like a connoisseur. "This ain't real leather, y'know."

Sam stuck his hands on his hips. "Yeah, I know it ain't real leather. They were backed up on cows at the plant that week."

"That's funny, Sam. Almost as funny as your lapels."

"Hey—the lapels are off limits. Listen, I don't tell you how to landscape that jungle on your face, and you don't tell me how to style my jacket."

"Go easy, Sammy, go easy. And hey—I like the kid's hat. We had a ton of deliveries in Brooklyn this morning." Harry tapped the brim of John's hat with casual affection.

"Hey, watch out for that head. That's precious cargo."

"Cool your jets, Mr. Swanky. I was only bein' nice. What's the big deal, anyway?"

"Like I said, this one's Special Delivery. I gotta keep him happy." Sprawled in the chair with his mouth half-open and his arms and legs spread out over the arms and footrest, John appeared neither happy nor unhappy.

"He looks like he's already delivered, if you ask me," remarked Harry with a flat expression.

Squinting, Sam approached John, knelt over and peered into his right ear. He then stood up, breathing a sigh of relief. "Nah, he's okay. He's fine and dandy in there."

"What do you mean?" asked Harry.

"What I mean is that I switched on a program installed in his head that's supposed to keep him occupied for the duration. Call it in-flight entertainment."

However entertaining the program running in mind, John did not initially experience it as such. Groping to orient himself, he found himself on the floor in a small dark room below a naked incandescent light bulb hanging from the ceiling by a single wire. Dim colored lights blinked feebly all around him, while a six-foot tall Van de Graaf generator sparked and crackled in the corner, giving the place something of a cut rate Frankenstein's lab feeling. Crumpled pieces of paper, spent fast food containers, banana peels, unopened utility and credit card bills, and a host of miscellaneous rubbish poured out from a dented gray metal wastebin like an active and very polluted miniature volcano frozen in time.

"Wait—this can't be. I was on the street and… what the hell am I wearing?" John realized he was suited up in an orange rayon top and green spandex tights, the garb of his comic book idol, Captain Whatever. This was one of The Captain's carelessly conceived outfits, whose color scheme was so repugnant that he was frequently reminded of how unappealing he looked, sometimes even in the middle of dealing with undesirables.

"Hey Captain, that outfit really has to go. Those orange and green duds are pathetic," a bystander strongly admonished the Captain as both dodged falling building debris all around.

"Can't you see I'm saving the planet? Piss off," replied the Captain, tossing city buses willy-nilly at his opponent, all the

while monitoring the latest results from the racetrack on his wrist Communicationalizer device.

"Okay, but once you're done with the bad guy and checking on the ponies, you should really look into some new threads. Besides, you got a split at your crotch that's getting worse," said the onlooker, pointing. "Nobody wants to see that shit."

Remembering this exchange from issue number 131, "Whatever-Ever Land," John regarded his costume with disdain. "I hate this outfit. But wait…" Scanning the tiny, barely-lit space, he further recognized his environs as the Cave of Indifference, the Captain's headquarters. "Why am I even here?"

"You're here because it was thought you would enjoy it, that it would be relaxing." A woman's voice interrupted John's confused ruminations. It was Gretchen, suited up as Captain Whatever's sidekick, *Ennui*. Ennui's outfit matched the Captain's, except reversed—her rayon top was green and the spandex pants were orange. She sat calmly on the edge of a gray industrial metal desk upon which also sat the Captain's three incongruously-sized computer monitors.

◐ ◑ ◒

Meanwhile, outside the realm of John's head, Sam was continuing to work out the details of the transaction. He spoke to Sam en route.

"Look, we all know that door up there ain't up to your expectations, sweetheart," Harry said. "But it's all we got. Everybody else is making do. We delivered a dozen of these already today and nobody else has made a stink like you're making."

"But nobody's got a Special Delivery like I got. Sure, if it was any old job, I'd say 'Fine. Just give me the door, maybe I can use it afterwards for when I build a guest entrance to my pool house, and toodle-loo to you.'"

"Toodle-loo to who?" asked Stu.

"Toodle-loo to…agh, never mind." Sam turned away slightly and then back again. "What I was trying to say was that when I could really use a nice regulation portal with a great shimmering entrance, glowing frame, glorious surround-sound stereo system, etcetera etcetera, you bring me this cut-rate piece of crap." He gestured disapprovingly toward the door and shook his head, punctuating his disgust. "I tell you the boss ain't gonna like it."

"Then the boss should make sure the factory is running at a hundred per cent and quit messing around with all the other bullshit everybody knows he's messing around with," said Harry.

"Hey, what the boss does with his time is the boss's business," said Sam. "And he's got a lot on his mind right now,".

"Then maybe he's so busy that he won't notice that you took the kid in with this door," said Stu.

Sam waved his hands in a show of defeat. "All right. Gimme what you got. And if it's not too much trouble, I hope you boys can help me getting the chair and my guest through this sweet little portal of yours."

"No problem. It's our last stop of the day, so we can spare a few minutes," said Stu.

"Thank you, oh kind sirs."

"Are you being a sometimes-funny prick again?" asked Harry.

"Oh no. I was being a speaking-with-the-utmost-sincerity prick this time."

Harry shook his head. "Well, all right. Let's get this done."

"And why are you here?" asked John of the woman in his company.

"I am here to be at your side," she said.

"I get that, being you're my 'sidekick.'" John flashed the double quotes sign with his fingers. "So I'm guessing this is a dream."

"Not really, but if it makes you comfortable please consider it as such."

"Well there's a heartwarming speech if I ever heard one. And are you supposed to be my girlfriend, Ennui, or both?"

"I would say 'both.'"

"'Both' doesn't really have the right ring to it, you know? 'Hey Both—come on down here and let's vanquish us some evil!' Nah. And since I am in no way ready to accept you as Gretchen, I'm going with Ennui."

"That's acceptable."

"It is? Well gee, that makes me really happy then."

"Really?" she asked in earnest.

"No."

Ennui drooped her shoulders in disappointment. "Well I do wish it were so. It was thought that the trusted accomplice of your favorite super-hero as portrayed by your beloved life partner would provide for you the ultimate edification."

"Gee, that's some strategic planning on the part of somebody. But no thanks. I'm good." John got to his feet, and walked a slow circumference around his companion's seated form. "Not that I would object to a little edification, mind you. You know, I was starting to become accustomed to the mystery voices, but this takes things to a whole new, unedifying level. First I get bounced all over the street by a guy with fifty-foot arms, and now... this." John fully circled the desk, and was now standing in front of Ennui again. Without warning, he launched his hand with his fingers straight out into her midriff, expecting to find she was a hologram of some sort, and that his hand would pass right through her. As the area was one hundred percent more solid than anticipated, his fingers plowed straight into her belly. Ennui crumpled in pain, dropping to the floor as if shot. John's face lit up with panicked fear and concern.

"Oh my god—what did I do? What is going on here? Are you okay?!"

"You nearly ruptured my spleen, you idiot!" The woman struggled to get out her words.

"But you're not real. I was trying to prove—"

"—that you're a masher? Christ." She took a deep breath. "Consider it proven. Help me up." Ennui held out her arm, which John grabbed as she gained her feet to stand in front of him.

"Are you okay?" John asked, almost tenderly.

With pursed lips and a stern look in her eye, Gretchen slapped him hard in the face.

John put his left hand to his cheek. "This can't be happening. Common sense says that none of this can be real," he said, taking a few steps away and shaking his downcast head.

"Of course it's not real, per se, John. But for the time being I would assume that it was, and that you treat me with respect."

"'Normally treat you?' I'm sorry, but I've never been with you before in a comic book—dressed in orange and green spandex, no less."

"The tops are rayon."

"Oh, how referentially inaccurate of me. I ask your forgiveness. Anyway, this is virgin territory."

"Then I suggest you draw on general previous experience."

"That's easy for you to say. You're an illusion."

"I'm as real as you'd like me to be."

"No you're not."

"Well then how about if I told you that Gretchen will be informed with the essence of how you treat me here."

"What?"

Ennui stood from her perch on the side of the desk. "I am drawn from her essence, and I will return there ultimately."

John sighed. "Well, that's super. But you know, as fascinating as all this is, essence of Gretchen-slash-Ennui, I think I'd like to go back to just hearing voices, if you don't mind."

"If you don't like this setup, I can make it look like some place else—"

"No, that's fine. If I'm going to be stuck in a hallucination with some sort of core of my girlfriend's being, it might as well be here."

"Whatever you like, sweetie."

"'Sweetie.' That is something—and I don't know how professional that is in terms of superhero-ing." He paused to regard the screens in front of him on the desk. "Well then, while we're here why don't we see how the Captain's computers function."

John reached over to tap the keyboard and wake the computer from sleep. On the three monitors were various maps and diagrams which at first glance appeared to be forensic analytical programs providing clues in tracking down villains in the Captain's home turf, Snoo City, but in fact were only still images of those programs at work.

"I think you missed a few details here," he said.

"We can fix that," answered Gretchen.

"What do you mean by 'we?' Who're 'we?'" asked John.

"Um, I can't tell you that."

"What else can you tell me, then?" he inquired further.

"That you're in passage." said Gretchen.

"In passage to where?"

"I can't tell you that either."

"Okay then—what can you tell me?"

"I can tell you that I love you."

John paused for a moment before responding. "Forgive me if I don't find that comforting, and I say that with as little sarcasm as I possibly can." John idly tapped his fingers on the desk, craning his head around to once more take in his surroundings. His eyes landed on a communication console on which screen featured two rows of four large rectangular buttons, over which there was a header that read **EMERGENCY CONTACTS.** The brightly colored buttons read **COPS, PIZZA, ARMY, CHINESE FOOD, PRESIDENT, BOOKIE, BEER,** and finally, **MOTHER.**

John gave a brief half-satisfied snigger of recognition. "Well, at least you got some details right."

◐ ● ◑

"Now we're talkin'." Energized at the prospect of getting on with the delivery, Stu clapped his hands and then rubbed them together quickly. Before attending to the door, he took a last, deep drag on his cigarette without subsequently exhaling even a wisp of smoke. He then flicked the end of the cigarette out onto the windshield of a nearby Pontiac. The butt bounced once on the glass and then came to a rest on the left windshield wiper, still lit. The driver of the Pontiac would later discover a curious charred area on one of his windshield wipers for which he would find no explanation.

Stu grabbed the door with two hands, and whipped it down to Harry and Sam on the street as if it weighed only a tiny fraction of its actual weight. Stu's sudden curveball toss nearly knocked Sam and Harry over, and they struggled to catch the door and land it gently on the street. The two men jostled back and forth to keep it upright, as if drunkenly sawing a huge log with a two-man crosscut saw. After a long minute of this queasy maneuvering, Harry and Sam were able to wrest the door to the ground.

Harry was the first to have words for Stu. "Hey! Next time go a little easy on the offload! You should know better."

Sam quickly followed with his own exhortation for Stu, who was leaning nonchalantly against the interior of the truck's compartment, his hands in his jean pockets.

"I do my best, Sammy," replied Stu, unmoved from his leaning position and now casually exhaling the smoke in letterform shapes from his cigarette of minutes ago to spell his name in the air, "S-T-U." "I do my best," he said after exhaling the "U."

"How many letters can you blow with one drag from your cigarette?" asked Sam, his hands on his knees and still heavily winded.

"I don't need a cigarette to blow letters," answered Stu, who then proceeded to finish his name in the air, shaping a "T" and an "U" in smoke out in front of him.

"Oh," said Sam, watching each letter evaporate in a burst as it hit an identical spot approximately four feet in front of Stu. "That's, er, a great trick you got there," he said nervously.

With one last deep breath, Sam stood up straight and then proceeded further with the examination of his delivery.

13

SHIMMER SHIMMER
KO-KO BOP

WITH THE DOOR SETTLED properly on the street and his composure regained, Sam stepped back from the door to inspect it in full. He circled it slowly several times before speaking.

"So, is there anything I should know about this thing before I use it?"

"Generally works like your regulation portal," said Harry.

"Do I need the balloons?"

"Nah. These units all came with them. Don't ask me why."

"I like the balloons," opined Stu. "They're cheery."

"'Cheery.' Sure." replied Sam. "You don't by any chance have a barbecue set to go with your Independence Day Special here, do you? We could get some hamburgers and hot dogs and have ourselves a nice little party."

"Stu, climb down and take the balloons off the unit for the gentleman."

Before Harry could finish his sentence, Stu had jumped down off of the truck and severed the multi-colored ribbons which tethered the helium-filled balloons to the doorjamb. The three men watched the balloons climb skyward.

"There goes the barbecue," remarked Sam. He then switched his gaze from the balloons to Harry. "Now what do I do?"

"What do you usually do?" replied Harry.

"Well, usually I set it up over here." He pointed to a nondescript spot in the road several feet away. "Could you, please?"

The two deliverymen grabbed the door, Harry on the left and Stu on the right.

"You ready, Stu?" asked Harry.

"Piece uh cake," replied Stu, who then nodded his head that he was ready to go to work.

With that, the two men moved the door to the general area where Sam had pointed. They put the door down, but before they could release their hands, Sam was on them with further instructions.

"Now over three inches," said Sam.

"What?" asked Stu, incredulous.

"Move it to the left three inches or it won't work."

"You gotta be kidding."

"Frequently I am. But not right now."

The men moved the door incrementally to the left, their eyes locked on Sam.

"Stop!" cried Sam. He executed his circling routine around the door and then two men, coming to a stop in front of them. "Great. That's perfect."

The men took their hands off the door, sighed in relief, and began to stand straight up.

"Now move it back five inches."

"What?" asked Harry. "You said it was perfect. This ain't funny, Sloan!"

"You want me to sign that 'RECEIVED' slip there on your clipboard, or not?"

Harry groaned and the two men lifted the door again, moving it backward, their eyes on Sam, waiting for his nod of approval.

"Okay. You got it."

"You sure now?" Harry said.

Sam circled again, leaning left and then right, gauging the door's position in relation to its surroundings. "Yeah I'm sure."

Harry sighed in relief, and Stu took the cigarette from behind his ear, lighting it with a flame that issued from the tip of his index finger. Simultaneously, a new cigarette appeared behind his ear.

"You boys really know what you're doing," offered Sam.

"Thanks," said Harry. "I hope we can use you for a reference."

Stu sniggered at Harry's remark, but the sarcasm was lost on Sam as he was completely focused on the portal. The man of the uncooperative lapels continued to examine the unit, moving his hands back and forth in front of and behind it, up and down and in random directions, as if trying to get a reaction out of it. Finally, he grabbed the doorknob and opened the door itself.

The view through the door stopped Sam dead in his tracks.

"Hey hey. What gives?" said Sam, perturbed.

"What gives with what?" Visions of pummeling Sam had begun to dance in Harry's consciousness.

"Where's the shimmer?" asked Sam.

"There is no shimmer," replied Harry.

"What do you mean 'there is no shimmer?' How can it be a portal if it doesn't shimmer? That's like a ham on rye without the ham."

"Look, I don't make these things. I just deliver 'em. Like I said, if you got a problem, take it up with your friend the boss."

"But how am I supposed to take the kid through this? He'll think I'm inducting him into some supernatural carpenters' guild."

"That's your problem. Besides, it looks like your kid has got enough going on with himself to worry about guild affiliations." Harry pointed to John, who was now leaning forward in the chair, and pensively scratching his chin in his slumber. "Yeah, he sure as hell sleeps funny," added Stu.

Inside the preternaturally activated recesses of his mind, John sat in the Captain's chair and leaned his right elbow on the desk, rubbing his chin.

"So now you're saying you can't make these computer programs work?"

"I'm not saying I can't," said Ennui. "It just wasn't part of the original preparations, and it would take some time."

"The 'original preparations,' huh? Interesting. Well then what were part of the preparations?" John spun around in the chair. "Do the Emergency Contact buttons work?"

"Yes. As far as I know."

"Well then let's see." John pressed the **BEER** button. At this point a loud "AROOO-GAH!" alarm sounded like something out of a World War II submarine battle. A six-pack of white cans with the red labels marked **BEER** floated down from the ceiling, suspended briefly by a tiny white parachute. The beer landed gently on the left side of the desk.

"I always thought that was unnecessarily showy," said John. "I mean, what's wrong with keeping beer in a refrigerator?"

"The Captain's preferences have been recreated as faithfully as possible," said Ennui.

"Well, nonchalance is one thing, but having beer drift down from the rafters is just silly affectation. Okay, let's see here..." John waved his fingers in front of the console before deciding upon pressing the red button marked **PRESIDENT**. "This should be interesting."

Upon pressing the button, a TV monitor began to glow to the left of the button console. From the glimmer, the face of a responsible-looking, middle-aged white man with neat, silver hair in a conservative blue suit and dark blue tie formed. The face on the screen addressed John directly.

"Hello John," said the man in the suit.

"Hello Mr. President," answered John.

"How are you doing?"

"I've been better, sir. I like to have some idea of what's going on."

"I know you do. I wish I could fully explain what's happening, but I can't. I'm sorry."

"That's okay. I wasn't expecting anything."

"Has Ennui been treating you well?" John looked over to find Ennui working to bring the partially-working computer systems to come fully online.

"Oh yes, sir. She's been peachy. People say you shouldn't mix business with pleasure, but seeing my girlfriend as a super heroine in spandex is definitely something I'll be putting in my scrapbook."

"You keep a scrapbook?"

"No."

The President paused. "Well, at any rate it's good to hear things are going well. And please continue to enjoy yourself. Think of this as a vacation."

"I don't need a vacation, sir. I'd like to get back to work, actually."

"There will be more on work very soon. In the meantime, think of the merits of being Captain Whatever. You can get all the pizza and beer you want, for one."

"That may be so. But to be honest, I enjoy Captain Whatever as a comic book, not as a lifestyle." John paused before continuing his chat with the Chief of State. "Sir?"

"Yes, John?"

"There is one thing I've always wanted to try."

"And what's that?" asked the President.

"This." John lurched forward and hit all eight emergency contact buttons over and over again as if engaged in a session of mad bongo playing, his hands flailing wildly all over the console. Sirens wailed, beer and pizza shot in all directions, every control panel light in the place flashed. A platoon of soldiers rushed in one end of the cave and out the other. John sat smiling in his chair, swiveling in it back and forth, following the assorted activity. He managed to dodge a personal-sized pizza, which came hurtling at him from behind the monitors, and crashed into the wall above the emergency contact buttons.

"I don't think you should have hit all those buttons at once," cautioned Ennui nervously, crouched next to John, her left arm shielding her head from flying pizza and framed photographs of Captain Whatever's mother. With her other arm she tightly gripped the right arm of the chair.

"Why not? I got direct orders from the President to enjoy myself. Can't disobey the Commander-In-Chief, now can I? And you know, a slice of pizza and a beer sounds pretty good right about now." Just then one of the desk drawers burst open, overflowing with steaming chicken chow mein.

"Don't try to change my mind," said John. "I'm not big on Chinese food anyway."

Outside of his head, John concurrently vocalized the same words, seemingly aimed at Stu, who was standing nearby.

"Hey Sammy—the kid just asked me for Chinese food," said Stu. "I ain't that kinda delivery guy."

"Hmm. There's something about this I don't like but I can't put my finger on it. We better hurry up. Let's get this done."

"Then sign here, here, and here," said Harry, proffering the clipboard to Sam and pointing to various spots on the attached sheet marked with a handwritten "X."

"You're sure this thing works?" said Sam.

"I've been delivering 'em all week and yours is the first complaint I've had, which I must say is not much of a surprise."

"Hmm." Sam rubbed his chin and paced back and forth in front of the portal.

Suddenly, Harry just missed striking Sam in the face as he thrust his arm out and through the door. Once Harry's arm crossed the plane of the threshold of the door, it disappeared as if plunged underwater. Yet there was nothing out of the ordinary to be seen on the other side of the door, unless you were expecting to see the rest of Harry's arm.

Harry pulled his arm into the visible world. "Satisfied?" he said.

"Yeah, okay," said Sam, with more than a hint of apprehension.

Harry shook his head, his displeasure mitigated by the prospect of nearly being finished with the delivery. "You're a pain in the ass. C'mon Stu."

The two men moved over to where John, sprawled in the chair, continued with his unconscious feast.

"I think you should wake him up," opined Stu, "That eating-in-your-sleep bullshit is freaking me out."

Sam put his hands on his hips and gave a John a long, hard look. "Cool your jets. He's all right—looks pleased as punch if you ask me."

"He looks punch drunk. I'd wake him up," said Stu.

Sam gave a half-shake of his head. "What're you, a broken record? And what am I gonna wake him up for, anyway? So he can get a good look at your Bob Villa special? I don't think so. I'll wake him up once we're through."

"It's your call. But whenever you decide his lunchtime is over you're gonna have to carry him separate. There's a weight limit," continued Stu, motioning toward the door.

"Since when does a portal have a weight limit?"

"Since now," interjected Harry, digging through papers on his clipboard to get to one at the very back of the stack. "It says here that there's a two person limit on this model. That chair alone weighs at least as much as two people."

"For the love of Shirley. And what else—do I have to show ID? Don't ask me to show my ID because I don't carry one. Never have and never will. If you don't trust me—"

Harry cut Sam off abruptly. "You don't have to show ID."

"All right, at least something is status quo around here. Now just help me get the kid and the chair through, and we're done." Sam went over to John and touched his head once more, instantly causing John to go limp in the chair.

"What did you do to him?" asked Stu, intrigued.

"I put him on pause."

"You can do that?"

"Yes I can do that, and I'll un-pause him once we're through. Now get him over by the door. I'll carry him the rest of the way on my back."

Harry thrust the clipboard in Sam's face, almost letting it drop before Sam caught it around his midriff. "Sign first. No more of your runaway trap. Shut up and sign or you can take your kid and your chair and shove 'em up your ass."

"That might prove difficult as my ass has a weight limit, fellas."

Sam and Stu stood motionless, their arms folded over their chests. His playful smile extinguished by a pair of baleful glances, Sam put his mark in the three designated places on the clipboard, and had barely finished doing so before Harry ripped it out of his hands and tossed it on the back of the truck. The two men then lifted the chair with John in it and carried it over to the portal. They jointly hoisted John up, each man under one of his arms.

"Where do you want him?"

"Just give him to me." Sam braced to receive his charge, taking on the additional weight with a slight grunt.

"Got him?" asked Harry, watching Sam waver back and forth under the grown man's heft.

"He weighs a lot for a skinny kid." After several moments of unsteady maneuvering, Sam was able to firmly stand, hunched over with John on his back, John's arms draped over Sam's shoulders. Meanwhile, Harry and Stu had turned the chair on its side and had angled it almost completely through the door. With a final shove, the chair disappeared into the nothingness of whatever was on the other side. Stu then moved quickly to jump back up on the rear of the truck, toss the clipboard back to Harry, pull down the liftgate, and jump back down off the truck to stand next to Harry.

"We gotta run," said Harry.

"Well, I ain't exactly got all day to go window shopping," replied Sam as John shifted in his sleep on Sam's back.

"See you next time, sometimes-funny prick." Harry and Stu started for the truck's cab.

Sam was about to enter the portal when he shouted to Harry. "And hey—don't forget to start up the city again. Last time you guys left everything standing still for a day and a half. Really screwed up the guys in Scheduling."

"I heard. Don't worry. They docked me a week's lunch and took away the Stu-ster's smokes. He was breathing fire like I've never seen before. Burned the friggin' dashboard."

With that, Sam tested the portal with his hand, saw that it disappeared just as Harry's arm had, and took a large step across the threshold with John in tow. Before he was completely through, Sam tapped John on the head again, which induced in John a brief, body-wide shudder of reanimation. Once they were through, the portal appeared to vanish into itself, and then it was if they were never there at all.

◑ *End of Part One* ◐

Made in the USA
Charleston, SC
07 July 2014